Other books by K.T. Dixon

Seminole Wind
Billy Brightpath
Volume I

Quicksand
Billy Brightpath
Volume III

Key Notes
A Collection of Folktales
From the Florida Keys
(short stories)

Don't Tread On Me
Billy Brightpath
Volume II

by:
K.T. Dixon

Visit K.T. Dixon on Facebook

Allusion Publishing

Where the Story Matters

This book is dedicated to all of those who stood by me through the most trying time of my life.

Special thanks to:
Kathy Holman, Pam Clark,
and Karen Stewart-Maddox

Author's Note:

We Southerners do things at a much easier pace than folks from other parts of the country, and that includes the way we speak. Political correctness has demanded the introduction of new words and phrases in American society to prevent people from feeling slighted or belittled, so it's no longer proper to say that someone speaks like a hick. Therefore, here in the south, we came up with an acceptable term to label our distinct dialect; "Southernese."

Southernese is not that much different than your normal everyday English, but there are a few alterations that need to be pointed out before you read any further. The first thing that you must learn is to drop the "G" from the end of most words. Example; when two people are having a conversation in the south, they are not talking, they're talkin'. And if someone is not going to do something they say, "I ain't goin'a do it." As you can see, we convert the phrase going to, into goin'a. We do that to almost every two word combination where the first word ends with "ing," and the second word is, to.

Of course, we still use our trusty old non-standards like ain't and y'all, as well as naw for no, and ya for you. We also like to throw in an occasional pause during conversation for dramatic effect, so you may find a comma scattered about here and there to create the desired effect. You know, to kind'a drive home a point.

Here endeth the lesson.

You're probably wondering why I took the time to explain my native tongue. Well, it's because you're about to take a journey back to the very heart of what Florida used to be, and you're going to meet a man that never left that place in time.

You can't get a language degree from one of those uppity Ivy League schools with this little lesson in Southernese, but you'll damned sure get a true sense of just how a good old boy talks and thinks.

Since you understand the lingo a little better now, let yourself ease into a southern state of mind. Mentally travel back to your favorite strip of beach on a perfect summer day and nestle down in the warm sand under the alluring tropical sun. Listen to the soothing surf lap at the shore and breathe in the salty air blowing in from the sea. Are you there? Are you ready to go? Now let that kindly old storyteller that brought you Seminole Wind slip back into your thoughts and offer up this next tale in the life of Billy Brightpath.

Enjoy,
K.T. Dixon

Birth of a Notion

The monthly meeting for the Free Brotherhood of the South got kicked off as usual; coolers were stocked with beer and foolishness filled the air. The group started back in the mid-1960s as the Glades County Klavern of the Ku Klux Klan at the height of the racial tensions during that era. Ever since their inception, the alliance met in an old two room hunting shack situated in the southern part of the Everglades. The owner and builder of the structure, Oscar Tatum, was the last surviving member of the original Klavern, and he left the place to the Brotherhood upon his death. The membership became more of a redneck social club after his passing and much less the hate based faction that the original founders intended. Once a month the membership gathered to get drunk, shoot swamp rats, and talk good old southern style bullshit, and that's the way it had been ever since Cletus T. Walker became a member twelve years ago.

Cletus T. is the quintessential, back country, southern gentleman. Being born and raised in Glades County, Florida, he's well mannered, respectful of others, and his personal views are basically conservative in nature. His thirty-two year old frame developed long and lanky throughout the years to fit the sultry South Florida environment. His skin is tough and tanned from the sub-tropical sun and his sandy blond hair is always scattered about. Cletus T. never got in a hurry no matter what the task. He always seemed to move in slow motion, the very embodiment of the laidback Florida lifestyle.

An influx of young Aryan believers spilled over from Miami a while back and changed the Brotherhood meetings dramatically. Cletus T. didn't care much for

1

the racial rhetoric that sneaked into his little fraternity, because one of his grandmothers was half Jewish and several of his lifelong friends are African Americans. Cletus put forth a motion to alienate the big city hate mongers at the last meeting, but it turned out that several younger members of the local chapter were deeply influenced by the immoral semantics. When the membership took a vote they refused to excommunicate the Aryans. Cletus T. felt betrayed. He immediately separated himself from the organization to start a less hate-filled splinter group and persuaded several of his colleagues to join the club.

The new band of brothers was most assuredly a redneck bunch, but they didn't have a prejudiced bone among their collective bodies. Most of them grew up in less fortunate parts of Florida, where neighbor depended on neighbor no matter the skin color, so taking a dislike to someone because of pigmentation never crossed their minds. However, being southern by birth, politics was right up there with football and religion when it came to the basic necessities of life. And that's where the new organization would take their fight; to the political arena.

The first meeting of the new group gathered in a garage at the home of Little Moe Gibbs, another former member of the Brotherhood and Cletus T.'s best friend since third grade. The group was a little cramped so they pushed Little Moe's broken down pickup truck out to the front yard and put it up on blocks to make thing more comfortable inside.

Cletus T. gaveled the meeting to order by banging a Black and Decker claw hammer against the surface of Little Moe's workbench. He welcomed all five fellow members to the new congregation and started things off by raising a cold beer to toast their new-found freedom.

After the consumption of several Budweiser tall boys, and a heated debate over the best quarterback in NFL history, the group got down to business and elect a president. Of course, Cletus T. was elected in a landslide, because he bought the beer that night. His first order of business was to devise a plan of action to motivate the new troops.

Sitting there half-drunk out of his mind with his ass hanging through the busted bottom of a wicker chair, Cletus T.'s inspiration came from a most unusual source. He labored to focus through inebriated eyes at the pyramid of beer cans the boys built, as the Southern classic, Sweet Home Alabama blast from the boom box sitting on the work bench. Cletus suddenly came up with a grand idea; it was time for the Great State of Florida to separate itself from the ever-demoralizing political forces of the United States of America.

Cletus struggled to pry his drunken ass from the busted chair, but he eventually made it to his feet and staggered to the makeshift podium. He picked up the hammer and slammed it down several times to call the membership to order. The hammer impacted the top of the boom box on the ninth whack and sent pieces of plastic rocketing through the air in all directions. The brothers stopped singing with the abrupt outbreak of silence and Cletus T. demanded their attention.

"Gentlemen, ya'll listen up now," he slurred with a thick southern drawl. "I got me an idea and I'm a thinkin' that ya'll should listen."

"Shut up and sit down," Junior Selby shouted at the others. "The president's wantin' to talk."

The boys got quiet and each of them took a seat. The air smelled of beer and cigarette smoke, but the mood quickly turned serious when President Cletus T. Walker started the political speech of his life.

"Boys, I've been a knowin' ya'll for quite a number of years. Other than riddin' the Glades of a few thousands swamp rats and a shitload of snakes, we really ain't done much to brag about, but all of that's about to change. I know that each and every one of you is a native born, God fearin', southern man. I myself am a direct descendant of the great Confederate General, Eustis Walker, and I know that you boys have southern blood a rushin' through your veins too. I'm here by declarin' that as men of Confederate ancestry, we ain't goin'a just sit around and take shit from a bunch of Yankee politicians anymore. I'm thinkin' that we should declare our independence and make Florida a free nation. We've put up with enough bullshit from Washington D.C.

"Like our freedom loving forefathers once demanded of their oppressive government, I say, don't tread on me," Cletus T. avowed.

The audience busted out with a big cheer as Cletus continued.

"Now, this ain't goin'a be an easy job, and it's just too big a task for one fella to do alone. So, as your newly elected leader, I'm callin' for a vote of this here body to see how many of ya'll are with me. When I call your name, say yeah if you agree, or naw if you don't."

"Junior Selby?"

"Yeah!"

"Little Moe?"

"I'm up for it."

"Jeb Cady?"

"Yeah man, let's do it."

"Bubba Wilkes?"

"Naw!"

Everyone in the group snapped their head around to look at Bubba. He was sitting in the rear of the garage near the beer packed refrigerator. "I was just funnin'," he said, opening the fridge to get another beer. "I'll do it."

Cletus T. laughed with the rest of the group and then called the last name, "Boo Hawkins?"

"Yeah," Boo replied. "Sounds like a plan to me. Throw me another one of them beers, Bubba."

"Alright then, it's anonymous," Cletus T. misspoke. He banged the hammer down twice. "We're goin'a split off from America. Now all we got'a do is figure out how we're goin'a do it."

The boys continued drinking and kicked around a few ideas on how to best handle their impending divorce from America. Bubba thought they should take the simple approach and send a letter to the President of the United States declaring their independence. At first that sounded like a pretty good strategy, but when the group realized that none of them could read or write very well, they just kind of let that proposal fade away with their sobriety.

Boo presented the motion to adjourn the meeting a little after midnight because some of the members had to work the following morning. Coincidently, this suggestion came up just as the last can of beer popped open.

During the discussion portion of the evening it was determined that beloved local hero, Dan Marino, was the best quarterback in history, and that racing legend Dale Earnhardt is still alive and well, and living on an island in the Caribbean with Elvis Presley and a bevy of beauties. A lot of nonsense came out of that first meeting, but amongst the foolishness one stroke of genius sneaked through; The Sons of the New Confederacy was born.

● ● ● ● ●

Cletus T. woke up the next morning just five minutes before he was due to clock in for work at the marina. He jumped into his clothes from the night before and rushed out to the driveway, where he found his pick-up truck parked directly on top of Cletus Junior's bicycle. A puddle of fluid leaked out from under the vehicle overnight and Cletus T. dropped to his knees to survey the damage. He was so drunk coming home from the meeting that he raced through the front yard, never seeing the bicycle lying in the grass. Cletus dragged it underneath the truck and came to a stop in the driveway just inches shy of impacting the house. The drunken process resulted in a small hole being punched in the engine oil pan and most of the precious fluid leaking out during the night.

Cletus opened the garage and rolled out a two ton floor jack with the speed of a NASCAR pit crew. He quickly jacked up the truck and pulled out the bike, then crawled underneath to wipe the oil pan clean with a gasoline soaked rag. Cletus T. dried the gas with the cuff of his shirt sleeve and put three layers of duct tape over the hole to stop the bleeding. Then he went back into the garage to retrieve a milk carton filled with the old oil drained from the engine during his last self-administered oil change. Though the used oil was burned out long before he changed it, it was the only lubricant available.

Speeding north along State Highway 29, Cletus T. had the king of all hangovers. Running twenty minutes late for work, he still took the time to stop at the Circle K on Azalea Street for a free cup of coffee. Bubba Wilkes owned the store, and Cletus always stopped in during his morning commute to get a caffeine fix.

Bubba woke feeling like he'd been kicked in the head by a mule, so he called his sister Scarlett to fill in for him at the store that morning. She knew that Bubba was feeling bad because he'd been out drinking with the boys, and when Cletus T. walked in the door, Scarlett unloaded on him. "What the hell do you want?"

"Damn woman," Cletus replied, strolling around the counter toward the coffee pots. "Hold it down a bit, please. I got a headache."

Scarlett fired back even louder. "I hope you die, you piece of shit. It's your fault that Bubba got drunk last night. Now, I'm stuck here all day instead of going out on the casino boat to play slots."

Cletus T. rubbed his throbbing forehead beneath the bill of his greasy old Evinrude Outboard Motors ball cap. He poured a Styrofoam cup full of coffee with his other hand. "All I want is some java. Will you let me get it and go, without all the screaming? It's like you're my damned ex-wife or something."

"Just get your coffee and get out," Scarlett demanded. "That'll be two bucks!"

"What? Bubba never charges me for coffee."

"Well, thanks to you, he ain't here. Now pay for it or go without it."

Cletus T. walked around the counter and dug into the right front pocket. When he pulled his hand back out and opened it, Cletus had a partial roll of Tums, an empty condom wrapper, half of a Viagra, a big wad of pocket lint and a dollar and fifty-two cents in change. He poked at the coins with his finger and mumbled, "I don't think I got enough."

"Just give me what you have and go," Scarlett said. "Get the hell out's here. You smell like a bucket of chum."

Cletus T. dumped the change on the counter and

picked up the cup of coffee. He started for the door, but stopped to look back at Scarlett. "When are we goin' out again?"

"You're shitting me, right?" she replied.

"Just thought I would ask," Cletus said, then nonchalantly went out the door.

Cletus T. always thought that Scarlett was a beauty. She was a little chubby, but by no means too heavy. He used to tell Bubba that she is just big enough to be fun in bed, and small enough that a man could walk with her on his arm in public; the perfect size for a real man. Scarlett was a pretty woman, but she had a baby eight years earlier and didn't lose all of the weight gained during her pregnancy. Like Cletus T., Scarlett had an ex-spouse, but she never found the right guy to hook-up with once the bitter emotions from the divorce passed. The two of them actually had a little fling a few years back, but Scarlett felt that Cletus T. was too immature to get seriously involved with, and she was right.

Sharon Walker divorced Cletus five years earlier. She took college courses on the internet to get a nursing degree and completed the clinical portion of her studies at a Miami hospital. Sharon stayed on there after getting her diploma, but the drive back and forth across the state was just too much of a hassle. So, when Cletus T. got busted on a minor drug charge, she had the out that she'd been looking for and made her move to Miami. Before he made bail on the charge, Sharon packed up her things and took off with Cletus Junior in tow. Cletus T. wanted to fight for custody of his son, but his attorney advised him that it was a waste of time with the pending criminal charge, so he decided to go with the court recommendation of bi-weekly visitation rights and tried to make the best of the situation.

Cletus accepted a plea bargain on the drug charge

and he was ordered to serve thirty days in jail. He actually only spent seven days behind bars and then finished the remainder of his sentence on probation.

The caffeine kicked in about half way to work and Cletus T. recalled the events from the previous evening a little more clearly. He still felt that Florida's secession from the Union was a good idea, but he had to figure out a way to do the job. Cletus knew that if the group was going to pull off this thing they would need a lot of money. All morning long he thought about nothing but the best way to get his hands on a bundle of cash in short order.

Cletus T. walked out on the pier behind the shop to have lunch and gaze at the beauty of Chokoloskee Bay. He sat down on the deck to let his feet dangle over the water, while munching on a peanut butter sandwich left in his tool box the week before. It was the kind of day that put the psyche at ease and stirred the imagination. The water was calm, the sky blue, and a gentle breeze blew onshore from the Gulf of Mexico. The Lady Luck Casino ship eased by offshore and Cletus T. grinned when thoughts of Scarlett came to mind. Then slowly, that kindly southern smile turned into a devilish grin.

"That's it," Cletus proclaimed to a pelican sitting nearby. He hopped up and hurried into the shop to make a phone call. Cletus T. told Little Moe to pass the word to all the boys that their presence would be necessary for an emergency meeting later that evening. And as president of the group, he ordered that everyone be sober when they arrive.

The meeting got kicked off a little after nine o'clock that night. Cletus T. hammered the membership to order and offered up his second suggestion as Commander in Chief of the new Confederate Nation of Florida. "Gentlemen, I think I've come up with a pretty good way for us to raise the money we need to ensure our independence. We're goin'a rob the Lady Luck Casino boat."

Boo Hawkins spit a mouth full of beer all over Junior Selby sitting in the chair in front of him. "Are you out of your ever-loving mind?" Boo shouted. "There ain't no way we can pull off a job like that."

"Sure we can," Cletus T. replied. "All we got'a do is make sure that we have the right people doing the job. That's why I'm appointing Junior here, Secretary of State. Everybody knows he's the brains of this outfit. And, I'm making Little Moe the Admiral of the Navy, 'cause he's got a boat. I'm pretty sure that we're goin'a need a boat to do the job."

Little Moe was surprised. "I only have a bass boat. We can't catch an ocean liner with that."

Junior Selby interrupted, "That's not goin'a be a problem. The casino boat only travels about ten knots when it's cruising. If we have a fast enough boat, we can catch it."

Cletus T. reassured his new admiral. "I know your boat can do it, Little Moe. I bored out the block last year and put them racing pistons in it, remember. It can do seventy-five miles an hour with no trouble at all."

"That's plenty fast," Junior told the group. "Now all we have to do is figure out how to get the money off the ship."

Jeb Cady sat quiet and listened for a while, but finally stood up to get the floor's attention. "I know what we can do, stick a bomb to the side of the ship."

"Capital idea," Cletus declared. "But where are we goin'a get a bomb?"

Jeb smiled and said, "We'll make one, and I know exactly how to do it."

· · · · ·

The New Year's Eve cruise of the Lady Luck Casino was filled with excitement. The big ship stretched four hundred feet from stem to stern and stood five decks above the waterline; she was the pride of the gambling fleet. The ship trawled ten miles off the Florida coast with the gaming tables filled to capacity. When the crew counted down and the clock struck midnight, the ship's horn blasted and the crowd exploded with a deafening cheer, but outside in the darkness another memorable event was just getting started.

A twenty-two foot bass boat came alongside the ocean liner with the accuracy of the Space Shuttle docking to the International Space Station. It eased up near the ship and got within twelve inches of the hull. Cletus T. reached out and attached a shoebox size package to the massive steel wall jutting up from the water. Little Moe then navigated the boat fifty yards away and set the throttle to keep pace with the ship. It took a few tries to get it right, but eventually the two vessels moved in unison like synchronized swimmers in the Olympic Games.

Cletus T. shouted, "Ahoy, Lady Luck. Ahoy."

A crewman working the aft deck onboard the ship heard the shout and spotted the little boat in the water below. He ran to the bridge to inform the captain of his sighting. "Captain Morgan," the deckhand shouted, coming into the wheelhouse. "There's a boat off the portside hailing us, sir."

"Where?"

The sailor pointed at the bandit vessel, "There."

Captain Jasper Morgan looked through a pair of binoculars and saw three men onboard the boat. One

11

held a black box with a chrome antenna sticking out the top, while another appeared to be armed with a shotgun. Knowing that the weapon could do little damage to the ship at that distance, Captain Morgan stepped outside the bridge and went to the railing. The ship's spotlight illuminated the tiny boat and the captain called out, "Ahoy vessel, do you need help?"

"Naw sir," Cletus T. replied. "We want your money."

Captain Morgan was stunned. "You want what?"

Cletus T. raised the black box over his head. "I said, we want your money. This here is a remote control device. It's connected to a bomb that we stuck to your hull. If I punch this here button, the bomb will blow a hole in the ship big enough to drive a bus through."

"I understand," the captain responded. "What are your demands?"

Cletus flipped a toggle switch on the remote and the detonator button started flashing. "You must surrender all U.S. currency in your possession. You have ten minutes to put the cash in a lifeboat and set it adrift."

Captain Morgan returned to the bridge and ordered the communications officer to notify the Coast Guard. He then directed six deckhands to survey the outer hull from the railing down to the waterline. One of the deckhands rushed back into the bridge a short time later and told the captain that a package was spotted attached to the hull. It appeared to be a brown box with wires attached and an aerial sticking out of the top.

"Seven minutes," Cletus T. shouted.

The Captain called the ship's security chief and instructed him to have all the money onboard loaded into the blue canvas bags used for storing cash in the safe. Once that task was complete, the bags were to be taken to the portside cargo hatch where deckhands would load them into a lifeboat and lower it down to the water.

"Five minutes," Cletus T. called out.

Captain Morgan rushed to the portside railing. "Sir, your demands are being met, but it may take more time than you requested."

Cletus T. raised his arm and shined a flashlight at his wrist watch. "Ya'll take all the time you want, but if you take longer than four minutes and thirty seconds, you'll be working underwater."

The portside cargo hatch popped open with less than a minute to spare. The Rebel gang watched intently as the deckhands slipped an inflatable life raft out of the opening and lowered it to the water. As soon as the raft touched the surface, the speed of the moving ship left it drifting in its wake. Little Moe backed off the throttle on his boat and watched the Lady Luck move away in the darkness. As the ship got smaller in the distance, he navigated over to the raft.

When they got within arms' reach of the lifeboat, Jeb Cady grabbed one of the lines attached and pulled it closer. "Damn, there must be at least two, three hundred thousand dollars there," he said, shining a flashlight at the bags of cash.

"More like a half million," Cletus T. guessed. "Jump in there and toss me them bags, Jeb. We got'a be fast. You know that the Coast Guard's on the way."

Once the bags were onboard the bass boat, the Confederate buccaneers went straight to their well-prepared hideout to stash the loot and lay low for a few days.

The Lady Luck made a bee-line to the Port of Naples. When it got within a mile of the inlet, the Coast Guard ordered Captain Morgan to stop and drop anchor. The ship couldn't enter the harbor with the bomb attached to the hull, so the Florida Department of Law Enforcement sent an explosives expert out to dismantle the device.

The police boat came alongside the ship and the explosives expert closely examined the package. "Are you kidding me?" the bomb cop said. He jerked the exposed wires from the device. "This isn't a bomb, it's a fake."

The officer pulled the package from the hull and ripped off the brown paper wrapper. He opened the box underneath and found a magnet from a boat generator and a Confederate Flag with the Florida State Seal sewn in the red field. There was a note pinned to the center of the flag where the blue bands and white stars crossed diagonally from corner to corner;

This here is our declaration that we ain't goin'a be a part of America no more. From this day forward, we declare Florida to be a free and independent nation. If we ain't afforded the same respect as any other country in the world, there'll be more attacks.

Long live the great Nation of Confederate Florida.

The Sons of the New Confederacy

Culture Clash

Special Agent Elroy Higgins stood in the office break room having coffee with fellow agents and discussing the upcoming Orange Bowl game. A courier entered and handed him a parcel from the FBI's regional office in Atlanta, Georgia. Higgins opened the package and found orders to investigate the events that transpired on the high seas on New Year's Eve, as well as the note left by the perpetrators and the altered Confederate flag. Since the robbery occurred beyond the state three mile shore limit, local authorities had no jurisdiction and the investigation had to be handled by the FBI.

"Dammit," Higgins said, "there goes the Orange Bowl." His beloved University of Miami Hurricanes was going to battle the Nebraska Cornhuskers for the College Football National Championship in just four days.

Agent Higgins weaved his way through the maze of desks filling the squad room where the field agents worked. He occasionally called out the name of an agent as he passed their desk and asked them to follow along. When he made it to his private office at the back of the room, four agents were close behind and they followed him inside. "Come in please, and close the door," Higgins said.

"Folks, we've been handed an assignment and you will be accompanying me to Naples this evening. It looks like a white supremacist group robbed a casino cruise a couple of nights ago. They were outside state waters and it's fallen on us to get the job done. We'll be pulling out at five o'clock today, so go home and pack a bag for a few days out of town, then be back here fifteen minutes before five."

Higgins stopped one of the agents when the group disbursed. "Agent Reichmann, before we leave, I need all the information you can find on a group called the Sons of the New Confederacy."

Agent Casey Reichmann was the best in the business when it came to extremist groups. She came from a family of privilege and did modeling work during her college years to relieve the stress of a double major curriculum in criminal justice and psychology. Her shapely body and glamorous look was exactly what fashion magazines loved on their covers. Casey's honey brown skin was silky to the touch, and her exotic tropical aura made men beg for her company like a hungry puppy wanting a bone. She always kept her long brown hair pulled back in a ponytail and wore a pair of red framed reading glasses during duty hours. Like a sexy school teacher dressing down to keep from distracting her puberty charged male students, Agent Reichmann tried to hide her beauty. She wanted to be recognized for her abilities in the male dominated world of law enforcement, but her splendor seemed to reach out and grab any man that dared to gaze into her majestic brown eyes.

Reichmann made big bucks modeling and had a bright future in the industry, but law enforcement was always her number one priority, so she threw away the flash and cash of high fashion when a chance to attend the F.B.I. academy presented itself. After a few years with the Bureau, agencies all over the world sought her input on radical groups. If Reichmann had nothing when a request came in, she jumped into the task with both feet and soon had an unbelievable amount of information to pass on. It was her behind the scenes work that prevented a terrorist attack intended to destroy the Golden Gate Bridge. However, Agent

Casey Reichmann carried a guilt in her soul that can't be appeased, and it was those skeletons in the closet that drove her to do such a good job.

The Miami division of the FBI was made up of the best field agents in America. During his tenure as director of the South Florida Bureau, Special Agent Higgins handpicked the cream of the crop from other divisions around the nation. If an agent in another part of the country did an outstanding job, Higgins swooped in like a college football recruiter trying to sway a star player from the high school ranks. He brought along videos of the sun-soaked Miami beaches, complete with shots of the local beauties drenched in suntan oil, as well as scenes of him with many of the local sports stars and music personalities that live in the area. The recruited agent always showed up in Miami a few days later to let Higgins treat them to a night on the town. Amazingly, one of the local celebrities seemed to always show up at just the right time to join them for a drink or dinner.

If Elroy Higgins wasn't such a good cop, he would have been a damned fine used car salesman.

● ● ● ● ●

When the team gathered just before five o'clock, Agent Reichmann gave Higgins the bad news; there was absolutely nothing in any database about a group called The Sons of the New Confederacy. They were obvious a new movement and intelligence would have to be gathered from scratch.

The group traveled to Naples in two separate cars via the Tamiami Trail. The Trail, as the locals call it, was the first roadway cut through the harsh jungle of South Florida to connect the Gulf of Mexico with the

17

Atlantic Ocean. It was an adventure to travel back in those early days, and there are still very few signs of civilization along most of the highway to this very day, but at the intersection of The Trail and State Route 29, the agents found a little tavern with a Confederate flag flying in front of the building. Agent Higgins assumed it would be as good a place as any to get things started, so he pulled into the parking lot.

Higgins ordered the other agents to go on ahead to Naples and find a hotel, while he and Agent Reichmann went inside the tavern to check things out. The little redneck beer joint is the only tavern on The Trail between Miami and Naples. The flat roofed building wasn't much bigger than a double wide mobile home. It had no windows and the cinder block exterior sported a bland shade of brown paint that faded over the years. A huge outdated beer sign adorned either side of the wooden door on the front. The sign on the left was a four foot red circle with a white "92" proudly embossed in the center. The rusty old relic was an advertisement for Oertels 92 Beer, which hadn't been served in the place since the brewery shutdown in 1967. The sign on the right was almost as old, it was a huge black and gold metal shield with a broad white strip running diagonally from side to side. Inside the strip bold red letters read, Falstaff. That company stopped production in 1990, but at least the color scheme matches the ugly exterior of the building.

When Agent Higgins opened the door to enter, the stench of cigarette smoke rushed out to greet him. Hank Williams Jr. blasted from the jukebox and every eye in the house watched as he and Reichmann took a seat in a booth near the door. The air conditioning didn't work well so the atmosphere was a nicotine filled haze that glowed with pastel colors from the neon signs scattered around the walls. The slow moving ceiling fans swirled the pungent fog, but did nothing to actually cool the room.

A waitress came to the table and Agent Higgins ordered them both a light beer. Agent Reichmann stopped the woman before she walked away. "Hang on, I'll have a Jack kicker with that."

Higgins shot her a stern look and waited for the lady to walk away. "You know that we can't drink hard liquor while on duty."

"Chill out," Reichmann replied. "It's for appearances, not consumption. I'm trying to fit in. Does this look like a light beer crowd to you?"

Agent Higgins looked around the room and realized that they were overdressed. Almost everyone in the place wore blue jeans and work shirts, and the guys all sported dirty ball caps or cowboy hats. His green Polo shirt and khaki pants made Higgins stand out like a turd in a punch bowl.

Reichmann wore jeans, but they were of the designer variety, and her Garavani top cost more than what most of these people make in a week.

Higgins shook his head. "We're not going to get a damned thing out of these people, are we?"

"I wouldn't count on it," Reichmann answered.

The waitress returned with the drinks and sat them on the table. "Will that be all, or would you like a spot of tea?" she joked, making fun of the city slickers.

Agent Reichmann grabbed her wrist. "Hang on a sec," she said, then turned up the shot of whisky and swallowed it in one motion. "Bring me another."

Higgins was amazed. "You never flinched. How can you drink whiskey like that?"

"The trick is to be used to it," Reichmann replied.

The two agents made small talk and tried to appear

disinterested in their surroundings. Higgins looked around the room occasionally and saw eyes fixed on them from every direction. After about twenty minutes, one of the local yahoos had finally consumed enough liquid courage to approach. He was a nice looking guy, tall, slim build, clean cut, wearing a cowboy hat. Unlike most of the patrons in the place, his clothes were clean. "Pardon me ma'am, but if your dad don't mind, how about you and me have a little dance?" he asked.

When Higgins stood up and asked the man to leave, three men at the bar got up from their stools and glared in his direction.

"Sure," Agent Reichmann said. She took the man's hand and slid out of the booth. "It's okay Uncle Elroy, just enjoy your beer. I'll be back in a minute."

The man smiled and led Reichmann to a small dance floor near the pool table. When he turned to face her and moved in close, she grabbed his testicles with her left hand and squeezed. "I don't know how it works around here, Slick, but where I'm from it's rude to approach a lady in the company of the man she's with."

The man bent slightly at the waist and whimpered in pain, "Oh, no, please."

The three men watching from the bar busted out with a big laugh. If Agent Higgins had interfered, the fight would have been on, but since the lady took matters into her own hands, so to speak, it was okay.

Agent Reichmann eased her face close to the man so she could whisper. "Now listen, shit-kicker, my friend and I are going to sit over there alone and finish our beers and you're going to pay the tab. Is that clear?"

"Yes ma'am," he groaned from a grimaced face.

Reichmann intensified her grip on his gonads and stared him coldly in the eye. "Then we're going out to the parking lot and a few minutes later you're going to join us. Don't tell anyone that you're leaving, just pay our tab and come outside. If you don't, I'm going to come back in here and rip your balls off in front of your friends. You got it?" she asked, with a short, quick downward jerk.

The poor man nodded his head in agreement.

"Say it, redneck, say the words," Reichmann insisted, tightening her grasp even more.

"Yesssss, ma'am," the man squeaked in a high pitch tone.

Agent Reichmann let go of the family jewels and went back to the table, where Higgins sat awaiting her return. She picked up the shot glass and downed the second hit of whiskey. "Now we have a lead," she told him. "My new friend over there will be joining us in the parking lot for a conversation when we're finished. He even offered to pay for our drinks."

Agent Higgins chuckle. "That was a thing of beauty."

The three guys at the bar laughed as their friend limped back and carefully sat on a barstool. "Shut up, ya'll," he shouted. "That chick can kick all your asses."

The agents finished their drinks and went outside. A few minutes later the redneck walked out the door still hurting from the vise grip treatment. "What do ya'll want?"

"What's your name, cowboy?" Higgins asked.

"Stokes, Wilber Stokes."

Higgins flashed his federal identification. "Okay Mr. Stokes, get in the car."

"I ain't done nothing," Wilber insisted. "Why are you taking me in?"

Agent Reichmann opened one of the rear doors on the sedan. "We're just going to get you out of sight, so no one will see you talking to us."

Wilber got in the back seat and Agent Higgins got in to drive. Agent Reichmann shut the rear door, then went around the car to get in the front passenger seat. They traveled south on Highway 29 for a couple of miles and turned onto a sand roadway that ran deep into the thick foliage of the Everglades. After going about five hundred yards on the secluded road, the jungle surrounded them on all sides. Higgins stopped the car and got out to open the rear door so Wilber could step out. Agent Reichmann came around the vehicle to where the two men were standing.

"Listen, Mr. Stokes," Agent Higgins said. "I'm here because a casino boat got robbed a few nights ago. Have you heard anything about that?"

Wilber leaned back against the car and stuck his thumbs down in the front pockets of his blue jeans, leaving the fingers on each hand dangling out. "Naw sir, I ain't heard nothing about it."

Hiding the thumbs is a classic behavior for someone that's not being truthful. Both agents picked up on the non-verbal signal and knew that Wilber was lying.

Agent Reichmann entered the conversation. "Have you seen anyone spending a lot of cash recently?"

"No ma'am," Wilber replied, shuffling his feet.

"Call me Casey, honey. I really hated having to hurt you back at the bar, but your friends didn't give me much choice. Are you okay?"

"Yeah, I'm alright, I reckon. I take it you're a cop too?"

Agent Reichmann showed her ID. "Yes, I am, and I know that you're not being honest. Why don't you just tell us the truth so we can all leave here on friendly terms?"

Wilber reached up and rubbed his chin. "I don't know anything, honest."

Higgins was instantly upset. "Get back in the car, Agent Reichmann," he said firmly.

After the second indication that Wilber was lying, touching the face, Higgins got angry. He grabbed Wilber by the ear like a mother scolding a child and pulled him into the jungle. Higgins came back out of the thicket a short time later with his pistol in hand. He walked to the car and put his left foot up on the front fender, then raised his pants leg and stuck the weapon back into an ankle holster.

Reichmann rolled down the window. "What happened? I didn't hear a shot."

"Did you ever see The Godfather?" Higgins asked. He put his foot on the ground and shook it so the pants leg would cover the weapon.

"Yes."

"Then let's just say that I made Mr. Stokes an offer he couldn't refuse."

Higgins told Agent Reichmann during the drive back to the tavern that Wilber dropped a dime on one of his friends at the bar. The one with the beard, Junior Selby, had been throwing around a lot of cash recently. Plus, he's been out of work for over eight months.

Higgins entered the bar the second time with his ID clipped to his belt and his weapon strapped to his hip. The crowd inside had a different attitude than before. This time most folks looked away and a couple of them even tried to slip out the door. But to their surprise, Agent Reichmann was waiting outside with her gun drawn. She quickly turned everyone around and herded them back inside the building.

"Turn off the music," Higgins shouted, but no one moved.

Reichmann walked to the end of the bar and admired the 1950's vintage Rock-Ola Jukebox for a moment. Then she raised her pistol and shot a forty caliber hole in the glass bubble atop the nostalgic contraption. The bullet went directly into the heart of the machine and the music died instantly.

Higgins held his ID up high so everyone could see it. "Listen up, folks. I'm Special Agent Elroy Higgins of the FBI, and that young lady over there is Agent Reichmann. We have three days to clear up a case or I'm going to miss the Orange Bowl, and that would really piss me off something terrible.

"We're looking for Junior Selby. We know that he was here earlier, but now he's gone, so would anyone care to help speed up this process?"

The crowd stood still and no one said a word.

"Okay, I guess we'll have to do this thing the hard way," Higgins said. "Agent Reichmann, check around behind the bar and see if you find any bottles without labels. I'll bet my badge that there's some illegal liquor in this place somewhere. When you find it, we're going to padlock this joint and arrest everyone in here."

Reichmann started around the bar, but the bartender stepped in the way to halt her progress. She swiftly drove her right knee into his groin and the man fell to the floor. "Damn lady," he sobbed, "you got something against testicles?" The man curled up in a fetal position holding his crotch.

Agent Reichmann opened a door in the counter below the cash register and found a sawed off shotgun sitting beside a jug with no label. When she popped the cork from the top of the jug, the smell that rushed out was absolutely unmistakable, it contained a gallon of Florida's finest moonshine; untaxed liquor, a federal crime. She held the jug and gun up for Higgins to see.

"Reichmann, call 9-1-1 and get the local police over here," Higgins ordered with a cocky tone. "Let's shut this place down."

"No, wait," the bartender called out from the floor. "I'll tell you where he went. Just hang on a minute. Damn!" He struggled to his feet and coughed a couple of times so his balls would drop back down into his nut sack, then propped himself up holding onto the edge of the bar.

Agent Reichmann announced that the tavern was closed and instructed everyone else to leave. Higgins walked over to the bar and sat on a stool near the bartender. "Sir, you're facing two federal charges with the altered weapon and the illegal liquor. If you give me any bullshit what-so-ever, I'm going to lock your ass up and confiscate this dump. I really don't see the federal government wanting to keep this shithole, so we'll probably just bulldoze it down."

"Junior lives in Ochopee," the bartender said. "About four miles down the highway back toward Miami. He hangs out down in Everglades City with a guy named Little Moe. There's a gang of them down there that run together. I don't know any last names, but there's Junior, Little Moe, and some fella they call Cletus T."

● ● ● ● ●

The agents that continued on to Naples were called back to Everglades City. Higgins found a nice little waterside motel there named of all things, The Everglades City Motel. The motel is a quaint place that sits on the western shore of picturesque Lake Placid at the edge of the Everglades. It has clean rooms and a coffee shop that serves home-style meals from six in the morning to seven at night. Agent Higgins bunked alone, while Reichmann doubled up with the other female agent, Kim Winters. Agents Frank Parks and

Phil Hernandez, shared a third room.

Agent Higgins called a staff meeting in the coffee shop and handed out assignments for the following day. Winters and Hernandez were ordered to find Little Moe and Cletus T. in Everglades City. Since the local population is only about five hundred residents, with any luck at all the search shouldn't take too long. Higgins ordered Agent Parks to contact the motel management and have the unused twin bed removed from his room. Then he gave Parks the most important task of all, he had to contact the office back in Miami and have the Technical Support Team bring over and set up a satellite tracking system in the room. Higgins gave strict instructions; the monitor and satellite system used during the Brightpath case was to be installed right away. The video equipment actually had nothing to do with the case, Higgins just wanted to make sure that he had a decent television to watch the Orange Bowl if they were still in town on game day. The little nineteen inch TV in his room just wasn't going to cut it. Lastly, Higgins told Agent Reichmann that she would be going with him to Ochopee to find Junior Selby. He liked the way she handled the situation with Wilber at the bar.

The agents met for breakfast the following morning and then took off to fulfill their respective duties. Agent Parks got on the telephone and started his assignment before the plates even hit the table. Higgins made it clear that he wanted the video system up and running by dinner that evening or there would be hell to pay. After breakfast, Winters and Hernandez went to the Everglades City post office to speak with the postmaster, while Higgins and Reichmann hit the road and headed out for Ochopee.

Since Ochopee is only eight miles from the heart of Everglades City, the drive over only took about ten

26

minutes. The little unincorporated community isn't much more than a bump in the road along the Tamiami Trail, with its sparse population spread out over a hundred and twenty two square miles of wetlands. Very few folks actually live in brick and mortar homes. Most reside in mobile homes or small camper trailers, but the town does have one very famous tourist attraction; Ochopee is home to the smallest post office in the world. Stamp collectors from every continent come to get the town's official postmark. Its 34141 zip code is a cherished piece of memorabilia for philatelist the world over. The building is only seven feet by eight feet and it originally served as a storage shed for plumbing parts. When the town post office burned down in 1953, the building owner donated it to the U.S. Postal Service, and it's been operating in that capacity ever since. The place is actually so small that it doesn't even have a restroom.

Other than the post office, Ochopee has a general store with a gas pump out front and a bait shop inside at the corner of The Trail and Bass Lake Road. On down the highway a piece is the town's only contribution to the world of science, The Swamp Ape Research Center and Campground.

When Higgins and Reichmann arrived they went straight to the post office. The door was locked and a note was taped to it; *back in ten minutes, had to poop.*

"Unbelievable," Agent Reichmann said. "Where are we, Hooterville? Let's see if we can find Sheriff Andy and Deputy Fife."

Agent Higgins laughed. "Calm down, they'll be back soon. Besides, you have your sitcoms mixed up. Andy and Barney worked in Mayberry."

An elderly lady walked up and unlocked the post office door. The Agents followed her inside and she stepped behind the counter in the tiny one room building. "Good morning ma'am. I'm Special Agent Higgins, FBI. This is Agent Reichmann. We're hoping you can help us out with a little matter."

Postmaster Margie Glenn never made eye contact with the agents. "Mornin'," she grumbled. "Don't know what I could possibly do for you folks, but I'll help if I can."

Higgins stepped up to the counter. "We are looking for a man named Junior Selby. Can you tell us where he lives?"

Margie Glenn served as the Ochopee Postmaster for over thirty years. She knew every resident in town. But there was one minor problem, Margie got burned out on her job back in 1988 and requested a transfer to any other post office in America. The request was denied and she's been stuck in Ochopee ever since, so Margie wasn't too keen about the idea of helping federal officers. She knew that she had to give them Junior's address, but Margie didn't have to tell them where he actually resides.

"Can't say where the man lives," Margie said, "but his address is P.O. Box 13, Ochopee, Florida, 34141. That's his mailbox right there," she added, pointing to a post office box on the wall opposite the counter.

After a couple of more questions and some very short answers, Agent Higgins could see that he was going to get nothing from Margie Glenn. The search was almost at a dead end. Junior Selby didn't have a police record and there's no actual town to search. Other than going door to door, which would take months, there wasn't much to follow up on. Their only other option was a visit to the two local businesses in hopes of finding a lead.

The agents headed for the market and bait shop on

Bass Lake Road. They found the store owner and three local citizens passing the time of day like most do in these parts; talking about fishing and playing checkers. When Higgins showed his federal ID, the conversation shut down like a union worker on a lunch break. He may as well have been talking to the gas pump out front. The agents said their farewells and departed.

On the way to the only other business in Ochopee, Agent Reichmann offered up a suggestion. "Maybe you shouldn't show your ID. We aren't getting a thing when these people see that we're federal agents."

"You may be right," Higgins said. "We got one more shot at this thing, so we'll try it your way."

Higgins and Reichmann soon arrived at the Swamp Ape Research Center. The place is dedicated to the study of the Florida Everglades version of Bigfoot, the Swamp Ape. Just like its world famous cousin, the local version of the creature is extremely evasive and not very photogenic. The owner of the Research Center, Pappy O'Dell Butts, is the only person to ever video the mysterious animal and he has DVDs for sale to prove it. Also available for purchase is an array of still photos of the creature, T-shirts, coffee mugs, key chains, and playing cards all embossed with a likeness of the creature, as well as cuddly little stuffed replicas of the big smelly beast.

Agent Higgins pulled into the lot and parked near the door. Agent Reichmann got out of the car and walked around to the driver side. She took Higgins hand when he stepped out. "Just play along, we're a married couple on a business trip. You browse around and act like you're interested in everything but me. That should convince them that we're married. And make sure to let me do the talking."

When the happy couple walked in, Pappy Butts

greeted them with a jovial, "Howdy folks, and welcome." He sat on a wooden stool behind the glass counter, wearing a pair of faded Duck Head overalls with no shirt underneath. Pappy sported a black cowboy hat accented by a band of alligator teeth. He had a full beard and the look of an outdoorsman. A 1940s manual cash register set atop the counter beside a black rotary dial telephone from the Kennedy era. Inside the case was his pride and joy, the only known plaster cast impression of a Swamp Ape footprint.

"Good morning, sir," Agent Reichmann said. "This stuff just fascinates me like crazy."

Pappy Butts smiled. "You're a Swamp Ape advocate, are you?"

"Actually, Bigfoot, I saw one in Oregon last year while skiing. But of course, no one believes me."

"Ain't that the way," Pappy replied, shaking his head. "Funny how folks don't believe something just 'cause they ain't ever seen it. I never saw Abraham Lincoln, but I believe he was real."

Agent Reichmann pointed at the plaster cast. "Is that an actual footprint from the creature?"

"Sure is," Pappy declared proudly. He held up a DVD. "I took it myself, the day I got the video."

Reichmann called out to Agent Higgins, "Come here, honey, and look at this."

Higgins saw the plaster footprint and lit up like it was the Holy Grail. "Is that thing real?"

"Of course," Reichmann replied. "This gentleman recovered it himself. He even has a video to prove it."

"Just ten bucks," Pappy proclaimed, sliding the DVD across the counter.

Agent Reichmann picked it up and looked at the cover. "Oh my, I've got to have this. I'll also take a coffee mug and a key chain."

Higgins interrupted, "Sweetheart, if I'm going to find Mr. Selby and get those probate papers signed, you're going to have to stop shopping. He's going to inherit a lot of money, but he has to sign the papers by the end of business hours today."

"You say Junior stands to inherit some cash?" Pappy asked.

"Oh…, I'm sorry sir, I didn't introduce myself," Higgins said. "I'm Marvin Gardens. I work for Higgins and Reichmann, Attorneys at Law. Mr. Selby's great uncle in Tennessee passed away last week, and I need to see him about some unclaimed funds. We know that he lives in the area but not sure exactly where. We have to get his signature on the paperwork before five o'clock or the money goes to the state."

"Shucks, I can tell you where he lives," Pappy beamed. "His place is over in Frenchman's Marsh, up there off Wagon Wheel Road. You can't miss it. It's the only place out there.

"Where the road elbows you'll see a trail running off to the left that goes back into the marsh. Junior's place is about a mile up that trail. It's a little camper trailer painted up like Dale Earnhardt's racecar, all black with a big white 3 on the side. He says it's a memorial."

Agent Higgins paid for the souvenirs and shook Pappy's hand. "Thank you for the help, sir. Let's go, sweetheart."

Higgins and Reichmann took off for Junior's place. They turned off Wagon Wheel Road onto a sand roadway and followed it into the wilderness as far as the car could go in the swamp-like conditions. The trail eventually turned into ankle deep mud and Higgins had to proceed on foot, but eventually the footing even became treacherous and he had to stop. Higgins looked

31

around and found himself surrounded by thick forest. When he was about to give up and go back, Higgins spotted Junior's trailer through the trees. The little bullet-shaped Airstream sat on the only semi-dry piece of land in the marsh. Agent Higgins breathed a sigh of relief when he found solid footing. He approached the trailer and found another structure with a note stuck to the door; *gone fishing*.

●　●　●　●　●

Back in Everglades City the search for Cletus T. and Little Moe was going a little better than the one in Ochopee. The town postmaster had addresses for both men and the agents were in route to Little Moe's house in no time. Agent Hernandez knocked on the front door. Amber Lynn Gibbs, Little Moe's wife, snatched it open from inside. "Who the hell are you?" she barked.

Agent Winters stepped forward and presented her identification. "Good morning ma'am, we're from the FBI. Can you tell us if Morris Gibbs live here?"

"Not no more," Amber Lynn replied. "That no good some-bitch ain't been home in three days. He's out drinking with that bunch of no-goods he runs with."

"So it's normal for him to be away like this?" Winters asked.

"Naw, not this long, maybe a day or two at the most. He leaves me and these babies here alone, and I don't know if he's dead or alive. I'm fed up with this shit. He can just stay gone this time."

"Where does he work, ma'am?"

Amber Lynn laughed. "He ain't got no damned job, ain't had one in almost a year."

"These friends of his, do you know them, ma'am?"

"None of them 'cept Cletus T. Walker. I've known

32

him for years. Damn shame what came of that boy, he used to be the heartthrob of the county. Cletus was a star quarterback at Glades High School and colleges all over the country recruited him. Then he got drunk one night and crashed the new truck that the University of Alabama booster club bought for him. Shattered both knees, there went the football career."

Agent Winters took notes on a small pad. "Do you know where Mr. Walker works?"

Amber Lynn knew where Cletus T. worked, but she wasn't going to tell the cops. "Nope, all I know is he works on boats."

Agent Hernandez shot Winters a quick glance, then he asked Amber Lynn one more question. "Are you and the children okay, ma'am?"

"Yeah, we're fine."

Little Moe Jr. was three years old, and Amber Lynn held an even younger son in her left arm. She took good care of her children, but poor little Darrell, the youngest, was always getting his head knocked into door frames when Amber Lynn walked through them without paying attention to the clearance. Both children needed a good bath, but they were feed well and their parents loved them very much.

Agent Hernandez handed Amber Lynn a business card. "If your husband comes home, would you please ask him to give us a call?"

Amber Lynn took the card and slipped it inside the left cup of her black Harley Davidson halter top. "If he ever comes home, he's the one goin'a be calling the law, 'cause I'm goin'a knock a knot on his head." She slammed the door shut and locked it from the inside.

Hernandez and Winters went to the address they had for Cletus T. Walker. When they pulled up in front of the house, the agents saw the gouge torn in the yard from Cletus T. running over the bike days earlier, but when they knocked on the door there was no answer.

The day wasn't going well for either team. Higgins and Reichmann were at a dead end in Ochopee, while Hernandez and Winters hadn't done much better in Everglades City, but at least they had something to work with. Agent Winters called the Internal Revenue Service and discovered that Cletus T. worked at the local marina. However, a trip there also came up empty. The manager told the agents that Cletus T. took off for the New Year's holiday and hadn't been back to work since.

Bootlegger Cay

After pulling the heist, The Sons of the New Confederacy went straight to the tiny island of Bootlegger Cay in the Ten Thousand Islands Natural Wildlife Refuge. The refuge is a scattering of countless mangrove islands, backwater marshes, and twisted canals that cover several hundred square miles off the Southwest Florida coast. The islands are strewn about so chaotically that even the most experienced guides have been known to get lost in the region. The place kind of looks like God had some land left over after creating the world, so he crumbled it up like a cracker and tossed it into the Gulf of Mexico. It's the perfect place to go if your intentions are to stay out of sight for awhile, and that's exactly why Cletus T. and Jeb Cady established a hideout there before the robbery.

Jeb is known to be the quiet member of the gang and he's a perfect example of the old adage, a quiet man is a dangerous man. But it wasn't natural ability that made him so hazardous, that came by way of Uncle Sam. Jeb looked around Everglades City for a job after graduating high school, but he wasn't exactly the sharpest knife in the drawer, so finding employment became a rather strenuous undertaking in itself. After kicking around town jobless for a couple of weeks, he decided to look into a military career. Jeb walked into the Army recruiting office in Naples, Florida at the gullible young age of eighteen years. The recruiter fed him the tastiest bowl of bullshit that Jeb had ever heard. The sharp dressed lieutenant promised him that the military would take his raw inner talents and train Jeb to be a top notch engineer. That was all he needed to hear, Jeb Cady saw big things in his future. He envisioned himself being a well-trained, highly paid engineer making a fine living in the field of commercial construction. The recruiter didn't bother to mention that the poor slobs digging ditches with hand shovels in some far off land is officially classified an engineer in the U.S. Army.

After basic training, Jeb was promptly sent to the Middle-Eastern nation of Turkey to begin preparations for construction of a new military base. He soon found himself stomping around in a mind field, waving a hand-held metal detector back and forth trying to find unexploded landmines. One thing led to another and Jeb decided that if he was going to be the guy having to find and dig up bombs he may as well learn all he could about the damned things. He learned the most effective way to discover, defuse, dismantle, plant, and detonate, every explosive apparatus known to the American military. By the time his four year hitch was up, Jeb Cady was one of the best booby trap men in the armed forces.

Bootlegger Cay is one of the larger islands in the Ten Thousand Island chain. Its land mass is covered with towering Cypress trees being choked to death by Spanish Moss, thick mangroves, dense sea grapes, and a spattering of Scrub Oaks that make it impossible to see the island surface from the air.

Cletus T. pawned his pick-up truck two days before the robbery and gave Jeb the money to purchase the materials needed to properly secure the island from unwanted visitors. Jeb decided that the Russian made PMN-1 Landmine, often referred to as a Black Widow, should do the job quite well. He set out in search of the joyful devices and wasn't too happy about having to go through the Miami Aryans to make the buy. Jeb returned to the island with ten Black Widows and rigged them up along with various other booby traps all over the island. To go along with explosives, he constructed a few strategically located spear obstacles and a couple of pit type traps filled with sharpened Punji sticks in the bottom. If a man didn't know his way through the obstructions, there's no way he could get to their camp without being injured or maybe even killed.

● ● ● ● ●

Cletus T. and Jeb gave up trying to get an accurate count of the money a couple of days after the robbery. Every time they counted out a thousand dollars they got stuck and couldn't count any higher. Cletus finally came up with the idea of making individual stacks of one thousand dollars and then counting the number of stacks, but that didn't work out too well after they wound up with seventy-seven dollars extra and didn't know what to do with it. Jeb contemplated the situation for a few hours and came to the conclusion that they could use the extra cash as toilet paper, since Cletus T. forgot to bring any along.

The gang was having a good time hiding out on Bootlegger Cay. The rest of the Sons joined the high seas bandits after Junior's near miss with the FBI. The escapade became more like a camping trip than a run from the law. They drank beer, cooked on an open fire, and just had an all-round good time for the first few days, but the forth night out things took a turn for the worst. During the day a cold front moved in and after sunset the air became unusually frigid. The temperature dropped to a record low twenty degrees and a heavy frost set in. None of the gang prepared for such conditions. Cletus T. was the only one that had an actual sleeping bag, but it wasn't much comfort after the ground froze and felt like a slab of cold concrete.

Everyone was still awake at three o'clock in the morning when the sound of possible footsteps and twigs snapping came from the jungle. Fearing the authorities had discovered their hideout, Cletus T. sent Jeb to investigate. Jeb moved through the bush cautiously, flinching every time he heard another blunt thud. He stopped every couple of steps and shined a flashlight into the Cypress stand all around. As the light beam moved slowly from right to left, Jeb caught a glimpse of something dropping from the sky. Initially, he was frightened, then he saw it again and realized what was happening. The icy temperature made the resident Iguanas slip into a state of hibernation, and as a result they were falling out of the trees unconscious. "Damn, it's raining lizards," Jeb remarked. He poked one of the comatose creatures with a stick and nudged it with the toe of his boot. "Screw this, I'm going home. It's too damned cold to be out here."

The other guys were all huddled around the fire when Jeb returned. "What's making the noise?" Junior asked.

"The damned lizards are freezing and falling out of the trees," Jeb replied. "And we're goin'a die too if we don't get somewhere warm." He crawled into his frost covered tent and started rolling up blankets.

"What are you doin'?" Cletus T. inquired.

"I'm packing my stuff and gettin' the hell out'a here. I ain't freezing to death over money."

Little Moe jumped into the conversation. "You can't go home, the law's got'a be looking for us."

Jeb crawled out of the tent with a blanket tucked under his arm. "I don't give a damn. If I do get busted, at least it's warm in jail."

Junior didn't care much for one of the gang bailing out on the plan, but he figured a way to use the mutiny to their advantage. "Okay, Jeb, if you want to go back home, nobody's goin'a stop you. But at least keep your eyes open and see if the law is snooping around town looking for us."

"I can do that, I reckon."

Junior told Little Moe to take Jeb back to Everglades City and drop him off at the marina. He asked Jeb to meet them back at the drop-off point the upcoming Friday night and let them know if the coast is clear. If it was safe to return, the gang would go home on Saturday and put their secession plan into motion.

Little Moe and Jeb boarded the boat and took off for the mainland, while the remainder of the group huddled around the fire trying to stay warm. Cletus T. sat close to the blaze to warm his feet. He was an outdoorsman to the core, but if his feet got cold, Cletus T. was finished. Cold hands, cold ears, cold nose, no problem, but when his toes got numb, the man couldn't stand it.

Boo Hawkins wrapped up in a blanket and nestled down by the flames, he was out like a light and snoring in no time. Junior covered himself with a blanket, but there was no way he was going to sleep in the frosty conditions. He just sat by the fire shivering and cursed Al Gore over the supposed global warming that is destined to wipeout mankind. "Deceitful bastard," he grumbled.

Cletus T. looked around and didn't see the last member of the gang. "Where the hell is Bubba?"

"He grabbed five bucks and went to take a dump," Junior replied.

"He's been gone a long time," Cletus T. remarked. "You better go check on him, Junior."

Junior mumbled under his breath as he walked into the jungle. He'd just gotten comfortable by the fire, but Bubba had been gone for a while, so it was best that someone check it out.

Junior found Bubba lying on the ground about forty yards into the brush. His pants were down around his ankles and he was knocked out cold. Junior shouted, "Cletus T., come quick."

Cletus ran through the forest and met Junior on his way back to camp. He was dragging Bubba by the arms with his pants still down. "Damn, what happened?" Cletus T. asked.

"I don't know," Junior replied frantically. "Grab his feet so we can carry him."

The boys got Bubba back to camp and laid him by the fire. They saw that his penis was swelled and his testicles were extremely red. "Is he gettin' wood?" Junior asked.

Cletus laughed. "Naw, not in these temperatures, he ain't."

Junior carefully examined the appendage in question and about half way down the shaft he found two tiny holes. "Oh lordy, he's been snake bit."

Bubba never saw the six foot long Water Moccasin that he'd hunkered down over to do his business. When he squatted, the snake lunged upward and took a quick bite. The resulting agony shot through Bubba's entire body in an instant and he fainted without ever making a sound.

Junior freaked out. "What're we goin'a do? He might die."

"You got'a suck out the poison," Cletus T. shouted.

"What do you mean, I got'a suck it out?"

"Well, if you don't, he'll die. And I damned sure ain't doin' it!"

Junior offered up a suggestion, "Let's wake Boo and get him to do it."

When Cletus T. woke Boo and told him what he

had to do, Boo slipped a pistol from under his blanket and stuck it right between Cletus' eyes. "I ain't sucking nothing," he declared. "What is this shit, I'm asleep for fifteen minutes and you guys turn queer? Now, leave me alone and let me sleep. And don't be touching my butt neither. I'll kill ya, sissy boy."

Cletus T. and Junior knew what had to be done; one of them had to overcome their hereditary homophobia and save Bubba's life.

The Ink in Her Veins

Billy Brightpath had been hiding in the Everglades for four months on the night of the casino robbery. During all that time he never second-guessed his decision to blow up the Glades Sugar Corp office building to protect his family farm. What else could a man like him do under similar circumstances? His grandfather taught him to respect the land and defend it with all his might, and the military trained him to eliminate his enemies with extreme prejudice.

Through all of those nights hiding in the swamp Brightpath had only one regret, he missed Sara like never before. But as much as he missed her, she missed him even more. Sara Sinclair carried the guilt of breaking his heart for a long time after their initial breakup, but when Brightpath left town to join the military, the high tide of sorrow receded and her pain faded away with time. She had no idea that the shame lingered in her subconscious like a storm beyond the horizon. Then when Brightpath was forced to leave her the second time, the raging squall of degradation rushed ashore in her heart and Sara fell into a state of deep depression. Her body was still recovering from the gunshot wound inflected by Major Weldon Sparks and Sara's state of mind hindered the healing process. But a few weeks after Brightpath departed, her cell phone buzzed on the nightstand late one night, and the words in the text were the perfect medicine for her broken heart and confused mind; *I love you and miss you very much. With God as my witness, I swear that I will return to you my love. I hold you in my dreams every night and in my heart always. B.B.*

The message inspired Sara and got her mind back where it needed to be. She was back on the job at the newspaper a few weeks later digging up hard-nosed news stories in the mean streets of Miami. Sara was back in full swing and the city editor knew it. When the casino story broke, Chet Battle sent her to interview the ship's captain.

Captain Jasper Morgan was one of those guys that never really had much adventure in his life, so he was happy to answer all of Sara's questions in great detail. The Captain smiled from ear to ear and spoke with the speed of an auctioneer as he recounted the robbery. He even mentioned that the escapade would make a great movie, and of course, George Clooney should play the role of the sea captain. Sara frantically scribbled notes as the captain rambled on. After forty-five minutes, she cut him off mid-sentence to answer her cell phone. The call came from Chet Battle, he'd learned through a confidential source that the FBI was in Everglades City looking for possible suspects in the case. Chet wanted Sara to go there and check things out. She was more than happy to get in her car and speed away. Captain Morgan had begun repeating himself and the story changed with every rendition.

Sara arrived in Everglades City about an hour after making her escape. It took her just a few minutes to find the FBI command post in the little town. When she pulled into the motel parking lot and saw Agent Higgins' government issued sedan, Sara started to pass on the assignment, but instead she put her personal feelings aside and did her job. She got the needed room number from the desk clerk and knocked on the door.

"Come in," Higgins called out from inside.

Sara opened the door. "Hey, Elroy."

Higgins looked up from the paperwork spread over his desk. His heart almost stopped. He'd not seen Sara since the night Brightpath left them standing in the darkness beside Snake Creek. "What could I do for you?" he asked, trying to hide his enthusiasm with a hint of attitude.

"I'm doing a piece on the casino robbery," Sara replied. "Would you like to make a statement?"

"You know that I can't comment on an active case. If that's all you came for, you may as well leave."

"What else would I be doing here?" she asked.

Higgins smirked. "You could lead us to your boyfriend. I have warrants for his arrest. It would make a good story for your newspaper."

"I have no idea where he is," Sara said, "so let's just drop that and get back on topic. Will you talk to me off the record?"

That was the opening Higgins was hoping for. "You give me something and I'll return the favor."

"What do you want?"

"Billy Brightpath," he told her.

"Honest, Elroy, the last time I saw him was the night he got in that airboat and sped away."

Agent Higgins watched Sara closely. He could tell from her body language that she was hiding something. The man was a human lie detector. Higgins analyzed her every move, but somewhere during the conversation, he let his observation skills skew away from professional training and turn toward the realization that Sara was still one of the most stunning women that he ever saw. Her skin looked smooth and rich, like that of a woman half her age, and her dark suntan projected an exotic radiance that highlighted her natural beauty. "Okay, off the record."

Higgins told Sara that the FBI was looking for a link between the robbery and a group of men that went missing on New Year's Eve. There was no definite connection at the time, but after they found one of the men in question things would become more apparent.

Though Elroy Higgins slipped up and let his personal feelings enter the conversation, Sara kept her mind on business and noticed a name scribbled in the notes on his desk. She left the motel and went straight to the Department of Motor Vehicles in hopes of tracking down the name; Cletus T. Walker. Her visit to the DMV would have to be quick, because Sara had an engagement back in Miami later that evening that couldn't be missed.

● ● ● ● ●

Bubba woke up with a high fever and weak as a kitten. It was the first time that he'd been awake since the reptile induced disaster. "Dang, what happened?" he mumbled.

"You got snake bit," Cletus T. told him.

"Water."

Boo Hawkins opened a canteen and leaned down to help Bubba take a drink. "Take small swallows, don't gulp," he said. "How do you feel?"

"Like shit, man. I'm freezing. Get me another blanket."

Boo looked back over his shoulder at Cletus T. "We got'a do something fast, dude. His fever is through the roof."

Thankfully, Junior devised a way to extract the venom from Bubba's body without anyone having to do the dirty deed orally. If he hadn't, Bubba would have died for sure. The ingenious devise involved the use of a spare fuel line for the boat with a siphoning bulb built in and a roll of duct tape. Junior tightly wrapped Bubba's penis with the tape and left a small air pocket directly over the snakebite holes. Then he cut a tiny slit in the pocket and inserted the end of the fuel line. After securing it in place with more duct tape, Junior started squeezing the siphon bulb and created a vacuum inside the air pocket. This drew most of the poison back out through the bite holes, though some had already entered Bubba's bloodstream.

"We've got to get something to break his fever," Boo said. "The man feels like he's on fire."

Again, Junior put his mind to work and came up with the solution. He suggested that Little Moe and Boo go to town after midnight to get some Extra Strength Tylenol.

"How are we going to get anything that late?" Little Moe asked. "The whole damned town is shut down after dark."

"Do I have to figure out everything?" Junior shouted. "I don't care how you get it, just get it."

The gang cared for Bubba and discussed a plan of action to secure the needed medication. Eventually, zero hour was at hand. Little Moe and Boo hopped in the boat and took off for the mainland. As they approached the dock in Everglades City, Little Moe shutdown the engine and used the electric trawling motor to silently ease into a slip at the Riverside Marina. Once there, they went straight to a storage shed that Cletus T. told them about to procure a sledge hammer.

The two insurgents quickly hiked the half mile to the pharmacy on Broadway and used the hammer to bust a hole in the back wall. Little Moe kicked through the inner sheetrock to crawl inside and Boo scurried in behind him. When they flipped on the flashlight, there before them was row after row of medical supplies. Boo lit up like Howard Carter discovering King Tut's tomb. "Oh man," he said with amazement, "you reckon they got any medicinal marijuana in here?"

"Dammit, Boo," Little Moe whispered. "That ain't what we're looking for."

Boo laughed. "It might not help Bubba's fever, but it'll sure make him not care that he's got one."

"Knock off the crap, man. We got'a get the meds and get out'a here."

The boys scanned the shelves for the needed medication, then rounded the corner to go down the next aisle. Suddenly, a blinding light stopped them dead in their tracks; "Police, freeze!"

The management decided to keep the store open twenty-four hours after the turn of the New Year, but of course, Little Moe and Boo had no knowledge of the extended service hours. When they started pounding the back wall with the hammer, the store manager ran out the front and came around the building to see what was making all the noise. He saw Little Moe banging away, then rushed back inside to call the police. The responding officer went to the stockroom and turned out the lights to await the perpetrators illegal entry.

Little Moe slowly raised his hands and sighed, "Dang."

Boo didn't say a word, he just turned, put his hands on the nearest shelf, and spread his feet apart to assume the customary position.

"Little Moe, Boo, is that ya'll?"

"Yeah, who are you?" Little Moe inquired.

The officer shouted for the store manager to turn the lights on. When the room lit up, the boys saw their longtime friend and fellow Elks Lodge member, Rollo Bartlett, pointing a pistol at them.

"What in the hell are ya'll doing?" Rollo asked.

Boo grinned and took his hands off the shelf. "Thank heaven it's you, Rollo. For a second there, I thought we were in trouble."

"You are, Boo. I'm the law right now, not your buddy. I got'a lock you boys up."

"Awe shucks, Rollo, come on man. We're just gettin' some Tylenol for Bubba. He's been snake bit."

"I'm sorry, but I got no choice," Rollo said. "Now put your hands behind your back and don't give me no trouble."

Officer Rollo transported his two friends to the police station for booking. When Little Moe put his hand on the computerized finger print scanner, the information instantly went to FBI headquarters in Washington, D.C. A message popped up on the screen; Attention: hold this individual for questioning. FBI agents are in route.

At Last

Billy Brightpath was out of his usual environmental element. The hotel room was dark and the pillow-top mattress felt much better than the sleeping bag that he'd slumbered in for the last few months. Brightpath eased out from under the thick comforter and made his way to the sliding glass door. He pulled back the drapes and slid the door open, then stepped out onto the balcony to gaze at the clear waters of Biscayne Bay.

The cold front that plagued Florida moved out to sea and the state returned to its natural sunny climate. Brightpath was greeted by a chamber of commerce day; a clear sky, pleasant seventy-one degrees temperature, and a rising sun that momentarily blinded him. He drew in a deep breath to taste the sea air and looked down at the white sand beach eight floors below. A local beauty strolling in the ankle deep surf captured his attention. The splendid lady cupped her hands together and dipped them in the ocean, then she raised the double hand full of seawater to her neck and let it stream down the full length of her superb body. Brightpath never witnessed a more pleasing site in his life. When he smiled at the vision of loveliness, she smiled back. He waved and Sara returned the gesture, then she teasingly turned to expose the profile of her shapely derriere in the tight swimsuit.

Brightpath laughed and nodded in approval. It was already the most wonderful day of his life, and she just made it even more enjoyable with her terrific sense of humor. Sara motioned for him to turn around. When he did, Brightpath found a fruit plate and a flask of coffee sitting on the balcony table. A pink post-it note was stuck to one of the cups; *I know you need the coffee to wake up, but make sure to eat the fruit. You're going to need the strength when I get back to the room.*

Brightpath lived in heartbreak for most of his life and during that time nothing was truly enjoyable, music had no rhythm and nature had no reason. Now, looking at Sara, the pain was gone at last. He recalled the many wonders experienced during his journey through life and their beauty finally found its way into his soul; the towering waterfalls of the South American rain forests, the dancing sands of the Middle-East, and the natural ice statues of the Northern Ukraine. Many breathtaking spectacles presented themselves to him over the years, but not one held awe until now. Being with the woman he loved was like seeing all the wonders of nature for the very first time.

They didn't plan their little meeting, it just kind of happened, with a little help from his cousin Abby and their friend James Osceola. Brightpath decided that it would be best to abandon his Everglades sanctuary when the cold snap hit, but the weather wasn't the only factor involved in the decision making process. He'd been battling a strong hankering for barbeque ever since leaving Louisiana, so Brightpath combined the two needs and decided to go live a comfortable lifestyle until the weather broke. Returning home was out of the question. The FBI had been watching the place ever since he disappeared, and there was nowhere in a little town like Deem City that would be safe, so he called Abby to ask for her input.

Abby suggested a trip to Uncle Nate's Bar-B-Q in Coconut Grove, and a stay at a nice beachside hotel she knew about just down the road from the restaurant. The transportation arrangements were made with the help of James, and Brightpath walked into the recommended restaurant at seven-thirty the following evening.

Uncle Nate's is world famous for its smoked ribs.

The place was packed with patrons when Brightpath arrived. He kindly asked for a booth near the kitchen when the hostess greeted him and the young lady was happy to accommodate his request. Brightpath told her it was so he could smell the food being prepared, but actually it was to ensure an easy escape out the back of the building if the law showed up. The dark paneled walls, huge wood burning fireplace and stone covered columns projected a log cabin ambiance, and the food was exactly what the palate was craving. His meal was unexpectedly interrupted. "Excuse me sir, may I join you?"

Brightpath looked up and couldn't believe his eyes. "Oh my god," he responded. He jumped up from his seat, wiping barbeque sauce off both cheeks with a napkin. "What are you doing here?"

Sara put a hand in the middle of his heaving chest and pushed him back down in the booth. "Hang on there, Chief. Sit back down and finish your dinner. But make sure that you don't eat too much, because as soon as you're finished, I'm going to take you somewhere and eat your clothes off. I expect full reciprocation."

Brightpath was happier than a hungry gator in a puppy mill. He wanted to grab Sara and start dining on her inviting neck right there, but instead he harnessed his desire and played along. "I have a lot of food left, this may take a while."

"I'll give you fifteen minutes," Sara said. "After that, we're going to box up those ribs and go find a hotel room. Then, I'm going to rub sauce all over my body and make you lick it off."

Brightpath sprang up again and yelled, "CHECK PLEASE!"

The evening started out with a man's simple desire for a good meal and a warm bed, but it ended exactly the way that destiny always intended. Though the barbeque sauce never made the bill of fare back at the hotel, Sara and Brightpath made love late into the night, then held each other until sleep overtook their exhausted bodies. The love that was caged for so long was free at last, and two fulfilled souls slept in peace as one.

● ● ● ● ●

Higgins took his time driving to the Everglades City police station. Agent Reichmann made an impression on him and he was acquiring a personal liking for her. They chatted over breakfast, had a few laughs, and then drove the short distance to the station at a snail's pace.

The police station looked like a throwback to the good old days of law enforcement. The building was an old gas station that had been converted into a police facility after the city received a ten million dollar grant from the Department of Homeland Security. It was actually filled with all of the modern-day technology necessary to ensure top-notch police work, but the building itself and the people that manned it were an accurate reflection of the easy-going community. The station consisted of a lobby and reception area just inside the front door, the chief's office in what used to be the first maintenance bay, and a squad room for the officers in a second bay. A booking area with two jail cells now occupied the former tire and auto parts storage room. The federal agents entered and Higgins asked the receptionist if he could speak with the Chief of Police. The nice young lady behind the counter told him that the chief was busy walking the dog of a local resident who was out of town on vacation.

"We found it," Agent Reichmann remarked.

"What?" Higgins asked.

"Mayberry," Reichmann replied. She turned to the receptionist. "Is Deputy Fife available?"

The young lady smiled. "Sure, hang on a minute." She picked up the phone and dialed the extension to the squad room.

A wiry young man with buck teeth came through a door behind the counter and introduced himself as Officer Amos Fife. He was dressed in a dark blue police uniform that looked three sizes too big, and Fife might have weighed a hundred pounds if he carried a brick in each pocket.

Reichmann glared at him. "Unbelievable. Is your name really Fife?"

"Yes ma'am," the officer answered with a country accent. "How can I hep ya?"

Agent Higgins presented his federal ID and told the officer that he wanted to speak with the prisoners. Fife led the feds to the jail cell where they found Officer Rollo sitting behind bars eating biscuits and gravy with Little Moe and Boo.

"Officer," Higgins shouted. "Are you armed?"

Rollo wiped his hands on his pants and pulled the pistol from his holster. "Course," he said, smiling.

Agent Reichmann drew her weapon and pointed it at the prisoners. "Freeze!"

"Jesus Horatio Christ, lady" Officer Rollo shouted. "Calm down, it's just Little Moe and Boo. They wouldn't hurt nobody."

"I can't believe these guys," Reichmann said.

Agent Higgins reached and put his hand over her weapon. "It's okay. Take it easy." Reichmann lowered her weapon.

Officer Rollo came out of the cell with a napkin tucked in the front of his shirt hanging like a bib. When Higgins told him to leave the cell block, Rollo dashed back in the cell to grab two more biscuits before going out the door.

Agent Higgins informed Little Moe and Boo of their constitutional right to remain silent, then told them that Captain Morgan had recorded the registration number on the suspect boat. He also told them that the boat was discovered at the marina earlier that morning and finger prints were recovered onboard that identified all of the suspects. He wrapped up the story and started the interview with a direct question, "Gentlemen, who is Cletus T. Walker?"

Boo's southern heritage kicked in. His Confederate convictions stepped to the forefront. He looked Higgins directly in the eye. "The only Walker that I know is a Texas Ranger, you federal piece of shit. I ain't saying another word until you get me a lawyer."

Little Moe was inspired by the rebellious words of his comrade. He jumped up from the prison cot and began a political rant that broke the case wide open. "You two are part of the corrupt political machine that's killin' America. Yeah, we robbed the ship, and we did it for every God-fearin', red blooded, patriotic Floridian. That money's hid so far back in them islands out there that you'll never find it. Now, kiss my ass!

"Long live the great Nation of Confederate Florida, and our beloved founding father, Cletus T. Walker."

Agent Higgins continued grilling the boys, but it did no good. They clammed up tighter than an oyster in ice water. He only assumed that Little Moe and Boo were involved in the robbery, but Higgins felt that it was a bluff worth playing. He also knew that he had an ace up his sleeve not yet played.

Jeb Cady was still sleeping when Agent Hernandez knocked on the front door. He rolled out of bed and stumbled through the house wearing just a pair of green plaid boxer shorts, a white tank top t-shirt and brown socks. Hernandez gave him time to put clothes on and then whisked Jeb off to the FBI headquarters at the motel. Higgins made him sit in the most uncomfortable chair that he could find and several minutes passed without anyone saying a word. The longer Jeb sat in the old hardwood, straight back chair, the more his butt hurt. When sweat popped out on his forehead, Agent Higgins knew that it was time to start the interview. "Do you know Morris Gibbs and Robert Hawkins?"

Jeb fired back. "You're shitting me, right? You had my sleepy ass dragged in here to ask that?"

Higgins stood up behind his desk and smiled. "I've been watching you for the last several minutes, Mr. Cady, and I can tell that you are hiding something. But that's okay, because I already know all about the casino job. We have Gibbs and Hawkins in custody, and they told us that you planned the whole thing."

Jeb jumped up from the chair. "You ain't got shit, G-man. If you did, you would've locked me up, instead of bringing me to this flea bag."

"What I have is your finger prints in the boat used during the robbery," Higgins replied. "And two men that swear you were a major player in the heist."

Jeb knew that Little Moe or Boo wouldn't rat him out. He was sure that they would go down alone before they snitched on anyone else. "Everybody in this town knows that I've gone fishing in that boat more times than you can count. And the last I heard, fishing is still legal around these parts."

Jeb pointed at the chair. "That chair is hurting my ass, so if you're going to arrest me, let's get to it. But if you ain't, I'm leaving." When he turned to leave, Agents Hernandez stepped in front of the door.

Higgins raised a hand and motioned for Hernandez

to step aside, but he asked one more question before Jeb got out the door. "Mr. Cady, do you know a man named Cletus T. Walker?"

"Sure do. He's the finest man that I ever knowed," Jeb proclaimed, then went out the door.

Agent Higgins put the pieces of the puzzle together very well, but after interviewing the suspects he made an assumption that couldn't be more wrong. Higgins believed that if Cletus T. was smart enough to pull off the high seas heist, then get away clean, he had to be a criminal mastermind.

Higgins went to the Riverside Marina later that day and chartered a guide that had knowledge of the Ten Thousand Islands. He, Agent Reichmann, and Agent Parks all boarded the vessel at noon and toured the labyrinth of islands until sunset. After cruising around in the tropical heat all day and finding nothing, Higgins came to the conclusion that a more effective method of searching would be necessary, so he shut down the operation for the night and went back to headquarters to make the arrangements.

Game Day

Agent Higgins was happier than a fat tick on a coon dog. He had two suspects in custody and a third one in his sights. He called the regional office in Atlanta, Georgia to have a search team dispatched to Everglades City, and since they wouldn't arrive until the following day, he readied himself for the Orange Bowl game scheduled to be played that evening.

Things were also starting to take a turn for the better out on Bootlegger Cay. Cletus T. and Junior were still worried about Little Moe and Boo not returning, but Bubba was feeling better after his fever broke during the night. He was up and around first thing in the morning making breakfast for everyone before the other boys woke up.

Of course, things were going even better on the east coast. Brightpath showered and readied for the day, while Sara put the finishing touches on the Captain Morgan article. When she called the FBI office in Everglades City to see if Higgins was ready to make a statement, he was out buying supplies for the upcoming sporting event.

Agent Reichmann answered the telephone. After Sara introduced herself, Reichmann repeated her name. "Sara Sinclair…, weren't you married to Elroy at one time?"

"Agent Reichmann, if you're fishing for info because he asked you to, you're wasting your time." Sara replied. "But if you're asking just to be cordial, then the answer is yes, I was married to him once."

"Please, call me Casey," Reichmann insisted. "Actually, I'm kind of attracted to him?"

Sara saw an opportunity and pounced. "I'll make you a deal, Casey. You give me what you have on the casino robbery, and I'll tell you something about Elroy that you would never imagine. And believe me girl, you want to hear this."

Reichmann was an FBI agent to the core, but she was a woman before she was a cop, so she couldn't wait to hear what Sara had to share. The conversation was all business at first, but that soon ended and the girl talk started. The two ladies connected on a personal level and that highly intelligent female bond kicked in; you know, the one that men can't begin to comprehend. The two of them chatted and laughed like they'd been friends for years.

Agent Reichmann said that she thought Higgins was handsome and witty, but he had trouble letting his job go and having fun. Sara agreed wholeheartedly. She gave Reichmann a few tips on how to loosen him up and trip his trigger.

"Are you sure that you don't mind talking about this?" Reichmann asked.

"There was a time when I truly thought that I loved Elroy, but all along I never did," Sara said. "Don't get me wrong, he's a good man, but when we got married I was screwed up mentally. I broke the heart of the only man that I ever really loved and was looking for a way to appease my guilt. Thank goodness, I got a second chance with the right guy."

"What's the scoop?" Reichmann asked. "What's the big secret that you're going to tell me about Elroy?"

Sara answered with a laughed, "Honey, I hope you like oral sex, because he loves it. And I don't mean you pleasuring him."

Reichmann responded with a giggle, "Oh my."

"He's good too," Sara emphasized. "The man can work magic with his hands. That's not to say he's lacking in other areas, just the opposite as a matter of fact, but he likes to make sure that you get the Big O at least twice before he even considers himself."

Reichmann responded with a joking tone. "To look at him, you wouldn't think that," she said. "I never saw a man whose clothes looked so bad on him. But that's part of his charm, he's so real and down to earth."

During her modeling days, Casey Reichmann dated millionaires, Hollywood actors, and some of the most stunning male models in the industry, but she never felt the excitement and inner satisfaction that she did in the company of Elroy Higgins.

● ● ● ● ●

The football game kicked off at 8:15 PM with Agent Higgins watched on the massive TV monitor that the tech guys mounted on the motel room wall. He had all of the male amenities necessary for just such an occasion; a six pack of beer, a bag of tortilla chips, a jar of salsa and twenty hot chicken wings. Disappointingly, the game turned into a lopsided affair. The Nebraska Cornhuskers led the Miami Hurricanes 38 to 7 at the end of the first half and there was no sign of a comeback. The Cornhuskers controlled the game from the opening whistle.

Higgins was miserable from the start, but he got even more pissed off when the halftime show started. The twenty minute production was a three million dollar extravaganza presented by Walt Disney World Orlando. During his one and only visit to the massive theme park, Higgins strolled around in the Florida heat all day and worked up a furious thirst for a cold beer. After checking several of the refreshment stands for a brew and finding none, he asked one of the attendants where a beer might be purchased. The cheerful young lady behind the counter informed Higgins that he would have to leave The Magic Kingdom to have an alcoholic beverage. He begrudgingly ordered a soda and the six dollar price was the straw that broke the camel's back. Higgins paid the outrageous price for the twelve ounces of watered down cola, then tossed it in a trash and headed for the closest exit gate, swearing off everything Disney for the rest of his life.

A gentle knock on the door interrupted his misery. Agent Reichmann eased it open without waiting for an answer. She entered wearing a body hugging Miami Hurricanes t-shirt that displayed every curve of her amazing torso and a tight pair of white denim shorts cut off Daisy Duke Style. Her silky brown hair draped over her ears and flowed down to cover her shoulders.

"Agent Reichmann, what can I do for you?" Higgins asked.

"Nothing really, I just wanted to watch the game. I heard it through the wall and was hoping you wouldn't mind."

"Not at all, please join me," Higgins replied very businesslike.

Higgins cleared the chicken bones scattered about the desk and offered Agent Reichmann a seat. Instead, she went to the bed and lay down on her stomach with her upper body raised and supported on her elbows. "Is it okay if I just stretch out and relax?" she asked.

"Sure," Higgins said, refocusing his attention on the game.

Elroy Higgins could read people like a book, but he totally missed the inviting vibes that Casey Reichmann sent his way. There she was, one of the most beautiful women in Florida, stretched out on his bed, sending every amorous signal in her arsenal, and it went right over his head like a gray bat on a moonless night.

Higgins paced the floor and began to accept his teams' coming fate. He occasionally stopped long enough to look at Agent Reichmann and grumble an unfavorable comment about the state of Nebraska. When the final whistle blew, she sat up and patted the mattress with her hand. "Why don't you come and sit down with me. It's just a football game."

"Just a football game," Higgins shot back. "People in Gainesville see just a football game when the Gators play. This is the Miami Hurricanes in the National Championship Game."

Reichmann stood up from the bed and stepped in front of Higgins to stop his pacing. When he looked into her eyes, her intentions were very apparent. "Agent Reichmann, I think it would be in both of our best interest if you left," Higgins said, with a jittery voice.

"Why don't you call me Casey when we're off duty?" She stepped closer and reached to playfully stroke his necktie. "Calm down, nobody knows I'm here."

Higgins caught a whiff of her aroma and gazed at her perfect lips. He imagined how magnificent they must taste. "The others, how do you know they didn't see you come in?"

Reichmann moved even closer. "Hernandez and Winters went back to Miami for the night, and Parks went to the Oyster House to watch the game."

Higgins got nervous. He'd wrapped himself up in work since the divorce and kept his sexual desires in check. He was the kind of man that refused to compromise his personal and professional standards for a few minutes of worldly pleasure. "I'm sorry, Agent Reichmann, but I must insist that you leave. I think it would be best if we both forget that this ever happened."

Agent Reichmann was disappointed to say the least. She did everything short of stripping down naked and throwing herself at the man. The federal agent was going to do as her supervisor requested, but the woman behind the badge refused to give up. Reichmann wasn't used to a man rejecting her advances, and that made Elroy Higgins even more desirable.

Higgins hadn't taken the time to notice the beauty of a woman in many years, but he did admire her attractive legs and exquisite bottom as Reichmann walked out the door. A part of him died after the divorce and female companionship was no longer a priority, but Casey stirred a sensation inside Higgins that he hadn't felt in over a decade. He savored the feeling as he watched her walk away, but once she was out the door a feeling of guilt filled his heart. Even though Sara had been gone for many years and he knew that they would never be together again, there was still a part of him that missed her very much. A void in his soul that he feared could never be filled, and the driving force behind his acceptance of everlasting loneliness.

Higgins lowered his head. "No man can control his heart," he whispered softly, then went back to his desk and buried the pain in work once more.

●　●　●　●　●

Sara finished the Captain Morgan article and sent it off for publication before she and Brightpath went out for dinner. They wound up at a nice seaside restaurant with a steel drum band playing on the outdoor deck. When the server came to the table and covered it with butcher paper, Brightpath took an instant liking to the place. He ordered a cold beer and a steak. Sara selected the seafood platter and a Rum Runner.

The drinks came and Brightpath asked if he could sample her beverage. A few minutes later, the server returned with dinner and he ordered a Rum Runner for himself. The setting was perfect, the music soothing and the drinks went down easy. Brightpath gulped down eight highball Rum Runners as the night progressed. Unfortunately, the tropical fruit taste of the potent cocktails hid the alcoholic dangers lurking in the glass.

Sara thought it was nice to see him loosen up and enjoy life for a change. She knew that he'd been living in the Everglades like an animal and needed a little party time. But her mindset changed when he jumped up on the table and started singing, Why Don't We Get Drunk and Screw, while the steel drum trio played the satirical Jimmy Buffett tune for the dining crowd. Sara was embarrassed and she tried to talk him down, but Brightpath just kept right on singing.

The restaurant manager came to the table with two bouncers and requested that they leave the premises. Brightpath initially had no trouble with the request, but things took an ugly turn in the blink of an eye. When the manager advised that he was going to call the police, one of the bouncers grabbed Sara by the arm to escort her out the door. Brightpath sobered up in a flash. "Let the lady go," he demanded.

"Just get out the door, asshole," the bouncer replied, jerking her arm.

The poor muscle bound moron never saw the punch coming. When his partner intervened, he too wound up on the floor knocked out cold. The entire physical altercation was over faster than a hiccup. The restaurant manager found himself facing a six foot two inch tall, rock hard, pissed off American hero.

"Please, mister, just leave," the manger begged.

Brightpath looked down at the little man shaking like a cold Chihuahua. "I want you to know that we weren't going to cause any trouble. I got out of line a bit and I'm sorry, but your man should've never touched the lady."

"It's okay, sir. Just leave."

Brightpath paid the bill and Sara drove them back to the hotel. She was going to lay a guilt trip on him about his behavior, but Sara knew that he would have never raised a hand if it were not in her defense. Brightpath was ashamed of himself. He felt about as low as an alligator's nuts, but Sara changed all that when she opened the hotel room door. "You know that I have to spank you for being bad," she said.

Brightpath saw a naughty smile cross her face. "Hercules times two couldn't whip my ass, what makes you think you can do it?"

"Because every Superman has his kryptonite, and yours is me."

The two lovers spent the evening exactly as both of them dreamed many times before. But like a wise man once said, all good things must come to an end. Sara awoke a little after three o'clock that morning and found herself alone. Brightpath knew that she would have to leave in the morning, and that neither of them was strong enough to say goodbye, so to make things easier he slipped out after she fell asleep. He left his spirit bag and a note on the pillow;

I'm sorry that I have to go like this, but we both know that it just can't happen right now. The longer I stay with you, the longer I want to stay, however the gods will not allow that at this time. I know that I don't have the right to ask this of you, but please wait for me. Our love is real and forever, and the spirits have told me that we will soon be together. Please carry this bag so it can protect you until I return.

I love you,
Brightpath

Sara stared at the bag and began to cry. She knew that she could wait a hundred years if necessary to spend just one more night like the last two. Sara pulled his pillow over her face to breathe in the remnants of Brightpath. It filled her heart with comfort.

While Sara cried herself back to sleep, Brightpath walked along a dark highway with his thumb in the air. A pick-up truck filled with farm supplies pulled to the shoulder of the road and he got in the passenger side door.

"Where to young fella?" the driver asked.

"Deem City, sir."

"It's your lucky day, that's where I'm going."

The driver was a nice gentleman in his late sixties. He liked to talk to pass the time. When the man asked Brightpath about the military attire, he channeled the conversation in another direction. The farmer didn't want to press the issue, so he started telling an amazing story about the time that he was robbed in Deem City. He wove an exciting tale about a naked man with several stitches in his forehead, robbing him of his clothes behind the Deem City liquor store a while back.

The Porcelain Altar

The search team arrived in Everglades City at noon and Agent Higgins briefed them on the current state of affairs. Their commander, Tom Moore, began his career as a cocky young military officer in 1973 and served up through the American police actions in Central America during the 1990's. When the U.S. turned its efforts toward the more desolate environments of the Middle-East, Tom decided that it was time to retire and take a job in the civilian sector. He accepted a position with a high profile private security firm in Washington D.C., and his first gig was pulling bodyguard duty for a well-known hotel heiress. The young lady attended a party at the ultra-upscale 9:30 Club one evening and Tom was assigned to be her wingman. Wherever she went during the event, Tom had to be within arm's reach for her protection.

Her stretch limo arrived at the club two hours late. The chauffeur hopped out to open a rear door and Tom stepped in to assist the heiress as she stepped out of the vehicle. She brazenly pushed his hand away and sashayed off to the specially prepared dressing room required in her twenty-five thousand dollar appearance contract. Tom stood quiet in the corner watching while a team of makeup artists worked vigorously to make the homely young lady appear somewhat attractive. She sat in an elevated chair in front of a brightly lit mirror barking orders the entire time, never once considering how hard the beauty technicians had to work to make her look glamorous. After thirty minutes of listening to her arrogant babble, Tom pulled a pistol from under his jacket and ordered everyone in the room to back up to the wall. He then lectured the young lady on how to treat people with respect.

The pampered princess had never been spoken to in such a demanding manner. She fired Tom on the spot. At first he took the dismissal with a grain of salt, but when the woman called him an ignorant, security guard, that was the worst mistake of her life. In a flash, Tom unfastened his belt and yanked the leather strap from around his waist. The next thing the little duchess knew, she was bent over his knee and it felt like the seat of her Coco Chanel britches was on fire.

Soon after his firing, Tom contacted a former Army chum that commanded the FBI search team. The friend offered him a position as technical consultant and the guy was promoted a short time after Tom came onboard. Tom took his place as commander and the rest is history.

The search team was made up of former military men and police officers from various departments around the country. They hung out together when on assignment and spent most of their off duty hours playing high stakes poker. The men had a standing bet during the games; if anyone could piss off Tom bad enough to make him walk away from the table cursing, they got a hundred dollar bounty from each player in the game. Tom Moore knew nothing about the bet.

When Agent Higgins took Commander Moore on a tour of the Ten Thousand Islands, they determined that the best way to search would be from the air. Higgins informed his supervisors in Atlanta and arrangements were made to have a helicopter flown in from nearby Homestead Air Force Base. A hot-shot U.S. Army pilot on special assignment with the Air Force received orders to report to Everglades City. He was issued a Bell UH-1c Iroquois chopper to do the job. The aircraft was a bit bigger than the one that he'd flown recently, but Captain Rick Hawks had a reputation for being able to fly any helicopter ever made through the eye of a needle without touching the sides.

Captain Hawks lifted off in Homestead at six-thirty that evening and flew into Everglades City a short time later. The Everglades City Airport is exactly what one might expect of a town with more critters than people. Its single runway stretches a half mile alongside the Chokoloskee Bay, there's a hangar that accommodates ten private airplanes, a control tower standing a staggering fifty-two feet tall, and a small restaurant that serves hamburgers and hotdogs, as well as beer and liquor by the drink. Rick introduced himself to the small town by buzzing the tower. He eventually sat the helicopter down near the smallest building on the airfield, because it had a Miller Lite Beer sign glowing in the front window. When Captain Hawks shutdown the engine and exited the aircraft, a security officer came running from the tower to discuss his reckless behavior.

As the officer wailed out and flailed his arms in anger, Captain Hawks walked by and casually tossed him his flight helmet and said, "Park it in the shade, pal. I'll be sleeping in tomorrow and I don't want her sitting in the sun."

The security officer went nuts. "Hang on a minute, asshole. I'm not a damned valet," he shouted. "Where the hell do you think you're going?"

"To have a drink," Hawks replied, never looking back. "And make damned sure that you don't change the radio station."

Captain Hawks strolled into the airport lounge like he owned the place. It brought to mind the little tavern at the Buck Head Municipal Golf Course where Hawks plays golf when he's back home in Georgia. He went straight to the bar to order a double shot of whiskey and asked to use the telephone. The bartender filled a glass with bourbon, then pointed to a pay phone on the wall. "Drinks are two bucks and the phone's a quarter," he said, apathetically.

Just when Captain Hawks started dialing the contact phone number in his written orders, Agent Higgins and Commander Moore walked in the door. "Captain Hawks?" Higgins asked, approaching him.

"Reporting as ordered, sir," Hawks replied.

"It's a pleasure to meet you, Captain. I'm FBI Special Agent Elroy Higgins, and this gentleman is Commander Tom Moore. We have a car waiting outside to take you to the motel for the night."

Hawks walked back to the bar and sat down on a stool. "If you don't mind, I just ordered a drink. Please feel free to join me, gentlemen."

Higgins responded sternly. "Captain, I have to brief you on the mission. I want to make it very clear that you only fly the chopper. No matter what happens, that's all you can do."

Commander Moore interrupted. "Hang on, Joe Friday. The man just asked us to have a drink with him. Where are your manners?"

"Okay, one drink," Higgins agreed, "but then we get to work."

Those were the last official words spoken that night. The lounge closed four hours later and all three men stumbled out the door drunker than a Billy Goat with a belly full of corn mash. Agent Higgins insisted that he drive because he had the least to drink. There was only one bottle of single malt scotch in the building, but there was an abundance of bourbon for Captain Hawks and Commander Moore to enjoy. When Higgins got behind the steering wheel, Hawks and Moore flopped down in the back seat and immediately passed out.

Higgins had trouble staying in the proper lane during the short journey as the car swerved freely from curb to curb. He tapped into his marksmanship skills to overcome the problem by closing one eye and aiming the vehicle down the middle of the road. When the car pulled into the motel parking lot and safely parked, Higgins turned off the ignition and breathed a sigh of relief as he opened the door. He then fell face first to the asphalt and promptly removed a sizable patch of skin from over his right eye. Struggling to his feet with blood flowing down into his eye, Higgins opened one of the back doors for Hawks and Moore to get out. After several unsuccessful attempts to wake them, he closed the door and retired to his room for the night.

Although the evening didn't turn out exactly as planned, overall it was a very productive day. Higgins had put together all of the resources necessary to begin the search the next day. But tonight the room was spinning and he was praying at the porcelain altar. The last thought to cross his mind before drifting into a state of unconsciousness was a question that many inebriated men have asked themselves over the years, "Am I going to throw up my shoes?"

● ● ● ● ●

Cletus T., Junior, and Bubba realized that they were in a fix. Little Moe hadn't returned with the boat and the food and water was running short.

"What the hell are we goin'a do?" Bubba asked the others. "We only got three hard boiled eggs and about a half-gallon of drinkable water left."

"I got no idea," Cletus T. replied. "Can you think of anything, Junior?"

Junior shook his head with frustration. "It looks like

we're in a jam, boys."

Bubba offered up a suggestion, "The water between here and home is only about chest deep. We could wade back."

An expression of terror adorned Junior's face. "It's at least two miles back to the mainland, and some of them channels out there are pretty damned deep. Ya'll are forgetting that I can't swim. And even if I could, the crocs would get us before we got fifty yards off shore."

Cletus T. looked at Junior. "I don't know why you're worried about crocodiles. We ain't ever goin'a make it off dry land. Jeb's the only one that knows where the booby traps are, and he ain't here."

Junior and Bubba never considered that little tidbit of information. "Damn, we may as well be in jail," Bubba remarked.

"We know there ain't no traps for a little ways to the north," Cletus T. said. He looked at Bubba. "That's the way you went when you got snake bit, and we brought you back with no problems. I say we go that way."

The boys headed north and made it to the spot where Bubba encountered the reptile. They stopped, looked in all directions, and didn't know where to go from there. Cletus T. suggested that they point in the direction of choice on the count of three. When he reached the magic number, each of them pointed in a different direction. Bubba was so flustered that he pointed back toward the camp.

Junior shouted, "Dammit, Bubba, we got'a go one of these other ways. Ain't no need in doubling back."

Cletus T. raised a hand above his head. "I guess that didn't work out too well. If you want to keep going north, raise your hand."

Bubba was still confused, so Junior raised his hand

to close the matter. Cletus said a few inspirational words to motivate his troops and then cautiously led them through the jungle. As he blazed a trail toward the outer shore of the island, Cletus T. unknowingly stepped on a low strung fishing line tied between two mangroves bushes. A tree limb sprang up amongst the thicket and a bamboo spear shot from the foliage. It whizzed by barely missing him. "Screw this," he shouted, "I'm going back."

"Hang on," Junior said. "We've already set off the trap, let's keep going. The water ain't much further. We just need to be careful."

Cletus T. contemplated the recommendation for a moment. "Alright then, just keep a lookout for anything that seems unusual."

The boys pressed forward with a determination that could only be failed by God himself or a massive explosion, and that's exactly what happened twenty yards ahead.

"That's it," Cletus T. screamed. He stuck his fingers in his ears and shook his head. The explosion deafened him and the ball of fire singed his eyebrows.

Bubba pointed at Cletus's head and yelled, "You're burning. Stop, drop, and roll. Stop, drop, and roll."

When Cletus T. dropped, Junior jerked the flaming hat off his head and started beating it on the ground. The fire was out after a couple of whacks. Cletus stopped frantically thrashing about and sat up. He yelled, "I'm deaf. Can ya'll hear me?"

Bubba leaned down and shouted a few inches away from his face. "Yeah, you okay?"

"Hell naw, I'm deaf."

Junior looked at the greenery all around and came to the conclusion that any further venture into the jungle might result in death. He pulled Cletus T. up from the ground and put the smoldering cap back on his head. "Come on, brother," he said, leading Cletus by the arm. "We can't do this. Somebody's going to get hurt."

The Return of Jeb Cady

Everglades City was fresh with the new day. The warm morning air carried a taste of sea salt in from the Gulf. Captain Hawks woke up on the backseat floorboard with his back bent the wrong way over the driveshaft hump and Commander Moore's butt resting squarely on his head. In that brief fraction of a second between his brain awakening and his eyes opening, Hawks thought surely he'd crashed a helicopter somewhere and woke up in the rubble. After gathering his faculties, he pushed Tom Moore aside and struggled to open the car door.

Hawks crawled out of the car on his hands and knees, then stood up to stretch, yawned, farted, and quivered from head to toe to shake off the night. "Damn, where am I?" he asked aloud, trying to spot a familiar landmark. He heard a voice call out, "Yo, help me out'a here."

The Captain turned and saw Commander Moore extending an arm out of the open car door. He grabbed the hand and pulled. "Man," Moore grunted, struggling to stand up straight, "we really tied one on last night."

"Yeah, wonder where tight ass went?" Hawks asked.

Moore pointed. "His room is over there."

The two hangover victims treaded softly on their way to room 102. After banging on the door a few times and getting no response, Commander Moore assumed that Agent Higgins must have awakened early and went for breakfast. When he and Hawks entered the motel coffee shop, Agents Reichmann and Parks were there, but not Higgins. Moore walked over to their booth. "Have you guys seen your boss this morning?"

"Not yet," Reichmann replied. "Did you check his

room?"

"Yeah, we knocked, but got no answer."

Agent Parks slid out of the booth. "We'd better check this out. It's not like him to sleep late."

The whole group went back to Agent Higgins room. Parks knocked on the door but he too got no response.

"I know he's in there," Reichmann said. "Let me open it." She reached into her pocket and pulled out a room key. Agent Parks shot her an inquisitive look as they all walked inside.

When the group entered the room they saw that the bed hadn't been slept in. Commander Moore called out for Higgins and a muffled groan came from the bathroom. The group rushed in and found Higgins lying on the floor with the side of his face pressed against the toilet bowl. Agent Parks knelt down to check his pulse. "Sir, are you okay? Can you hear me?"

"Of course, I can hear you," Higgins replied with his eyes closed. "You don't have to scream."

Higgins wiped the dried vomit off the side of his face as he slowly rolled over to sit up. He opened one eye and looked at his shoes. "Thank heaven, they're still there."

Captain Hawks laughed. He separated the group from the rear and stepped through. "You're going to be okay, killer. You just had a little too much to drink last night, that's all. Somebody go get the man a cup of coffee."

Hawks helped Higgins to his feet, then walked him to the bed to sit down. Commander Moore soaked a washcloth with cold water and pressed it to the back of Higgins' neck. After a couple of minutes, he became more aware of his surroundings. Higgins looked up at Captain Hawks. "Thanks, man," he said sarcastically. "I know you for two minutes and wind up like this."

Pressing his face against the cold porcelain toilet bowl all night made the muscles in the side of Higgins face numb. He couldn't open his left eye or move that side of his mouth.

Captain Hawks looked at him and laughed. "I was going to say that I've had worse effects on people, but I can't remember when."

After using the warm compress for a couple of hours, Higgins was back to a hundred percent and his entire face worked again. He, Hawks and Moore came up with a plan and put the wheels in motion. Hawks drew out a grid on a map of the Ten Thousand Islands, and a couple of hours later Commander Moore loaded his team in the helicopter. Captain Hawks dropped them off on one of the nearby islands so the team could familiarize themselves with the environment, while Hawks and Higgins took to the sky and began the hunt.

Captain Hawks looked down at the specks of land below. "We're never going to find anything like this," he said. "The jungle covering these islands is just too thick."

"We have no choice," Higgins replied. "It would take forever on the surface."

● ● ● ● ●

While the federal conglomerate did their thing, Sara Sinclair made her way back to Everglades City and started doing a little digging around of her own. The casino robbery filled the news since New Year's Day, but she wanted to do an article from a different point of view. All of the reports so far made the Sons of the New Confederacy sound like the biggest threat to the State of Florida since Hurricane Andrew, so Sara knew that if she interviewed the gang it would sell a lot of newspapers. She started her research at the Oyster House Grill by striking up a conversation with a local gentleman seated at the bar. He was an elderly man that knew all of the men she asked about, but like most folks in a small town, the man really didn't surrender much information to the stranger asking questions. While Sara talked to him and took notes, an eavesdropping waitress slipped into the kitchen to make a phone call.

An average looking man in his mid-thirties entered the restaurant about twenty minutes later. He took a seat on the stool beside Sara. "I hear that you're looking for Jeb Cady."

Sara looked up from her note pad. "Yes, I am. Do you know where I can find him?"

"That depends on what you want him for."

Sara introduced herself and explained that she wanted to find the Sons of the New Confederacy so they could tell their side of the story. This intrigued the man, so he asked a few more questions. Liking the answers that he got, he told Sara to meet him at the Riverside Marina in an hour, and told her to be ready to take a boat ride. Sara called Chet Battle to fill him in on the angle that she wanted to take the story and he loved the idea. He was a little worried about her going off with the stranger alone, but Chet knew that she could handle herself if things got tough.

Sara scanned the docks at the marina and saw the stranger loading a boat with bottles of water and boxes of food. "Excuse me, sir," she said, approaching him from behind. "It looks like you're planning on being gone for a while. I think I'll pass on the trip."

"It's up to you lady," the man replied. "But I'm Jeb Cady, and I liked your idea of telling our side of the story."

"Why didn't you tell me at the bar?" Sara asked.

"I had to have time to gather these supplies. I'm going to take this stuff out to the boys, so if you want to talk to them, get in the boat. You'll be back before sundown."

Sara sent Chet a text message on her cellphone and then boarded the boat. Thirty minutes later, Jeb eased the vessel into a narrow canal on Bootlegger Cay. He navigated inland and ran the boat aground mid-island. The two of them set out on foot from there, weaving their way through the jungle. When they stepped out of the brush into the clearing near the campsite it startled the others. "Hey guys."

"Man, it's good to see you," Junior said. "I thought you'd never be back. What's with the chick?"

"She's a reporter. She wants to talk to you guys. But she ain't all I brought, I got food and some bad news. Boo and Little Moe got busted. The FBI is crawling all over town looking for us. They're using a helicopter to search the islands."

Cletus T. couldn't believe his ears. "Are you out'a your dog-gone mind? Two of us got busted, the FBI is looking for us, and you bring a reporter to our hideout."

"It's okay," Jeb replied. "She can't tell anyone where we are as long as she's here. She was asking questions around town and I thought it was best to shut her up."

Sara got a bad feeling. "I just want to interview you gentlemen and get out of here. Don't worry, I won't tell anyone where you're hiding."

Jeb walked toward her with a length of rope. "You damned sure won't. You ain't goin'a get the chance."

Sara knew that she had to do something or she was going to be in a fix. She quickly stuck her hand in her shoulder bag. "I feel it would only be fair to tell you that I sent a message to my editor and told him where I was going."

Bubba yelled, "Dang, Jeb, now we're screwed."

"No we ain't. She might have told somebody where she got on the boat, but she couldn't have told them where she went. She ain't had the chance."

Jeb jerked the bag from her shoulder and tied Sara's hands behind her back. "Listen lady, I don't want to hurt you, but I will if I have to," he said. "Just sit down and don't try to run."

Sara could tell that Jeb meant business. His attitude was more intense than the other guys. Fortunately for her, she slipped the cellphone into her back pocket after texting Chet. It was still within reach. The distraction move with her hand in the bag worked perfectly.

● ● ● ● ●

The chopper buzzed the islands all day and found nothing. Captain Hawks sat the big Huey down just before sunset and joined Commander Moore in the airport lounge for a drink. Agent Higgins refused to join them for a second libation session, so he hopped out of the aircraft and returned to the motel.

Agent Reichmann was waiting for Higgins when he arrived. "I have news from our boys in jail. I offered them a deal and they confirmed that they have friends hiding in the islands."

Higgins chuckled. "After talking to those two it was pretty obvious that they didn't pull this job off alone. It's clear that neither of them are the brains of this outfit. I think this guy, Cletus T. Walker is the smart one. But we didn't see a single sign of human life out there in those islands anywhere."

Reichmann walked over to the kitchen counter and picked up a matchbook. She took one of the matches out and lit it. "If you were out there after dark, what is the one thing that you would make sure you had?"

"Of course," Agent Higgins said with excitement, and rushed out the door.

Higgins hurried back to the airport lounge where he found Captain Hawks still sitting at the bar. "Where's Commander Moore?"

"He left with some woman," Hawks told him. "Said they were going to a club up the road to have a few drinks and dance."

Agent Higgins called Moore's cellphone but it went to voice mail. He looked at Captain Hawks and asked, "Are you too drunk to fly?"

"I hate to disappoint you, sir, but after what you did to us last night, I'm just nursing a beer."

"Yeah, like that was my fault," Higgins replied cynically. "Let's go."

Hawks and Higgins boarded the chopper and took to the nocturnal sky. Higgins instructed Captain Hawks to take the helicopter up to a thousand feet and be on the lookout for signs of fire below. If the Sons were out there, they would certainly have a campfire burning at night.

The dark specks of land scattered about in the silvery sea reflecting moonlight were easy to see from overhead. Five minutes into the flight, Captain Hawks spotted an orange glow on one of the islands. It was obvious that something was burning beneath the trees. Agent Higgins looked down through a pair of binoculars. "Log our position, Captain. We'll start our search on that island in the morning."

Hawks locked their location into the GPS computer mounted in the instrument panel and then turned the airship around to go back to Everglades City. When the chopper made it back over the mainland, Higgins pointed out the windshield. "We're going to take a short side trip, go that way. I want to make damn sure that Commander Moore is able to work in the morning."

Higgins directed Captain Hawks on a flight path that took them on a course directly above State Route 29. As they neared the intersection with the Tamiami Trail, he pointed out the tavern below and told Hawks to land in the parking lot. The helicopter touched down between two rows of pickup trucks and the crowd inside the building rushed out upon hearing the noise. Commander Moore was among the masses that flushed out the door. He walked over to the chopper when Agent Higgins stepped out of the aircraft below the spinning rotor blades.

Higgins shouted over the engine noise. "We found the island, Commander." Moore slid open the starboard side cargo door and got inside the helicopter. Higgins climbed back into the co-pilot seat and the chopper lifted off. "Playtime is over, gentlemen," he said sternly. "It's time to get to work."

Commander Moore replied with his best Mr. Scott impersonation, "Aye, Captain." He and Hawks busted out laughing.

Agent Higgins couldn't help but laugh too. He knew that these guys could do the job now that the time was at hand. He could tell that by how hard they play. Higgins learned long ago that the harder a man works, the harder he has to play, so he was pretty sure that these guys were be the best in the world at doing their job. Higgins also thought that the search would be as easy as riding a bicycle now that they had the location, but he forgot that folks sometimes fall and break bones when they ride bikes.

Enter Our Hero

The mission kicked off at nine o'clock the next morning. The sky was bright blue and the wind was little more than a lazy breeze, but there was an uneasy calm in the air. Captain Hawks flew the helicopter just above the water with Agent Higgins riding shotgun as Commander Moore readied his team in the cargo bay. Hawks raised the chopper to clear the trees when they got within sight of Bootlegger Cay. "No way that's habitable," he told Higgins. "There's nothing but heavy brush down there."

Moore attached a metal ring on his utility belt to the steel cable coming from a hydraulic winch mounted inside the portside hatch. "Take us over the spot where you saw the fire last night and station the ship at thirty meters," he told Captain Hawks. "We'll drop down through the trees at that location."

"Roger that," Hawks replied. He positioned the chopper at the requested height and with his expert hands on the controls it froze in midair. Commander Moore swung out the hatch and hung in midair. He hesitated for a second to look down, then back at his team. "I'll go down and check things out," he said. "I want you guys to come down in fifteen second intervals after I give you the all clear."

The entire team flashed a thumbs-up. Team member Sonny Blake flipped the switch to activate the winch. Moore dropped out of sight below the chopper and down into the thick tree canopy below. A thunderous explosion blew a massive hole in the trees when Moore descended into the branches. The chopper shuttered like someone grabbed the tail and gave it a good shake.

"What the hell was that?" Higgins shouted.

"Up, now," Moore shrieked over the radio. "Take it

up. Up!"

Captain Hawks lifted the helicopter and Moore came into view above the trees. His pants were on fire and he desperately swatted at his flaming butt with both hands. "Reel me in, for Christ sake. My ass is burning."

Sonny Blake reversed the toggle switch on the winch to raise the cable but nothing happened. Blake frantically flipped the switch back and forth. "The damned thing's broke," he shouted. "Do something."

"Not a problem," Captain Hawks said calmly.

The chopper moved offshore and dropped down to the water below. When Commander Moore touched the surface, he was never more relieved in his life. "Thanks, Cap, I owe you one," he called out over the radio. "That was some quick thinking."

"You owe me more than one," Hawks joked. "It could have literally been your ass if I wasn't on my game."

Agent Higgins shouted to the team in the cargo bay, "You guys pull him in." Then he turned to Captain Hawks, "Let's go back. We have to re-evaluate this thing."

Jeb Cady did an outstanding job booby trapping the island. He wove a spider web of fishing line among the trees limbs that connected to two of the Black Widow Landmines planted in the Cypress canopy above the camp. This took an aerial drop completely out of play. A whole new strategy would have to be devised to reach Bootlegger Cay. The helicopter returned to Everglades City Airport and the team headed to the lounge for a cool beverage and a quick briefing. To ensure everyone's sobriety, Agent Higgins informed the bartender that alcohol sales were suspended for the duration of the meeting. Seconds later, Captain Hawks bellied up to the bar and ordered a beer.

"Sorry, the bar's closed," the bartender said. "You can have a cola or some water if you want, but no alcohol."

Captain Hawks pleaded. "All I want is a beer."

The bartender pointed at Agent Higgins. "Talk to the big cheese over there, he's the one that shut me down."

Hawks went to the table where Higgins and Moore were looking at a depth chart for the water around the Bootlegger Cay. He tried his best to convince Higgins that having a beer wasn't really drinking, but his efforts were futile.

After forty minutes of debate another plan was formulated and the group was in the air again. This time Captain Hawks would drop the search team in the shallow water near the island and they would wade ashore. Everyone knew that land based traps would be waiting, but Commander Moore was one of the best in the business when it came to evading such obstacles.

Hawks lowered the chopper to within inches of the water and stopped in mid-air. He looked back over his shoulder at the team and gave the order, "It's go time, boys."

Commander Moore hopped out and splashed the surface. The depth charts were right on the mark, he only sank waist deep. The remainder of the team quickly followed and they all waded to the island.

● ● ● ● ●

About the same time that the rescue team reached Bootlegger Cay, Billy Brightpath woke up at his Everglades hideout. He started a fire to brew coffee, then cut a hunk of alligator jerky off the naturally cured meat hanging on a nearby tree. Brightpath contemplated his duties for the day and decided that the first order of business would be a quick trip to Fort Banyan. James Osceola always left a load of supplies there on the fifth of each month, and today was the day.

Brightpath fired up the generator and plugged in his cellphone to charge. After two cups of coffee, he unplugged the phone, shut down the generator, then strapped on his gun belt and got in the airboat to start the journey. The sharp saw-grass standing just above the waterline leaned slightly with the slow moving current and warm breeze coming in from the Gulf of Mexico. Brightpath sped the boat across the surface and thanked the spirits for another wonderful day, but it would turn out to be a day that he wished never came. A day when he would have to put aside all thoughts of self-preservation for the good of the woman he loves.

When Brightpath got within range of a cell tower his phone buzzed. He slipped it out of the small holster attached to his belt and pressed the voice mail button. Brightpath listened carefully to the muffled voices for the full duration of the recording. He heard three male voices, but there was a forth voice that he struggled to grasp. He knew it was a female, but the audibility was just too stifled to make out clearly until just before the call ended, "Please let me go," he heard Sara beg.

Brightpath knew by the intensity in her voice that Sara was in trouble, and it was apparent that whomever she was talking to didn't know that she made the call. A feeling of urgency filled his heart. The blood rushing through his veins carried a rage to every part of his body and his mind clicked into military mode. Everything between him and his endangered love was suddenly at risk of annihilation. Brightpath knew that he had to do something, so he called Abby and told her to meet him at James Osceola's gift shop.

The Rolls-Royce powered airboat raced across the River of Grass at almost seventy miles per hour. Abby parked the truck near the dock behind the gift shop and she was standing at the tip of the wooden pier waiting for him to arrive. He eased the boat up to the dock and tossed her a line to tie onto one of the pilings.

"What happened, Billy? You sounded upset on the phone."

Brightpath stepped out of the boat and rushed to the truck. "Sara's in trouble."

"What is it? Where is she?"

"I don't know," he said, "but listen."

Brightpath played the voicemail for Abby and she heard a part of the conversation that he missed. She distinctly heard the name Cletus T., and the phrase Sons of the New Confederacy.

"I know what's going on," Abby told him. "This thing has been on the news the last several days."

"What are you talking about?"

"A group called The Sons of the New Confederacy robbed a casino boat, and Sara did an article about it. It was in the paper yesterday. I definitely heard someone use that name during the call."

"Are you sure?" Brightpath asked. "If that's what she's working on, then her boss will know where she went. Do you still have his phone number?"

"No, but I remember his name, it's Chet Battle."

"Good, we have a place to start."

Abby called the newspaper as soon as they made it back to the ranch. She filled Chet in on Sara's call, and he told her that Sara went to Everglades City to do a follow-up to the story. He also told Abby that the FBI was there and that Elroy Higgins is leading the investigation. She came out to the garage to give Brightpath the bad news. He was preparing his tailor made bulletproof vest for the mission. The garment served him well during his time in the military. The vest had five long, thin pockets on the right side to carry ammo magazines for his sidearm, three larger pockets on the left for rifle magazines, and three steel clips to attach hand grenades on each side of the brass zipper running up the front. After hearing the news, he told Abby to get Agent Higgins on the telephone.

White Feather swooped in and landed atop the pick-up truck just as she disappeared into the house. "Your freedom will be at stake if you go."

Brightpath looked at the white osprey that carried the soul of his grandfather. "I have no choice, Grandpa. Sara is in danger."

"Choices are yours to make as you will," his spirit guide said, "but you must remain free and alive if you are going to fulfill your true calling."

"If this is something that I feel must be done, then is it not a part of my destiny?" Brightpath asked.

"The Great Spirit will not allow me to disclose your path, that is something that you must discover alone," White Feather said. "However, I can say that you should not let the things of this world become a distraction. What you are about to do is for the good of one, but your true purpose will benefit many."

White Feather never led Brightpath wrong in the past, and though he knew that his grandfather's spirit was speaking by the grace of the Creator, Sara's safety was more important to him than any purpose that his own life might serve in the future. "I'm sorry, Grandpa, I have to go. I love her."

White Feather called out in a bold voice. "Then go, but know this, you will need all of your strength to survive what is coming. Do what you must and let the future be what you make of it today." The bird spread his wings and thrust himself into the air. It flew over the burned sugarcane fields and vanished in the distance.

Brightpath finished his preparations and slipped the vest over his massive arms. Pulling the zipper half way up, he left his bare chest exposed. He then slid an old steamer trunk from beneath a workbench and opened it. The metal hinges squeaked after years of neglect and dust flowed off the top like snowflakes down a frozen rooftop. Inside was an assortment of military hardware that he sent home over the years; an M-16 automatic rifle came back piece by piece, ten ammo magazines and hundreds of bullets, as well as two dozen M61 fragmentation grenades and twelve MK3 concussion grenades. Also in the trunk was the one weapon that Brightpath rarely held and never fired; a World War II vintage forty-five caliber, a 1911 model Colt pistol that White Feather carried when he served as a Windtalker during World War II.

Brightpath clipped three of each grenade to the front of his vest, then picked up the Colt and glared at the pristine weapon. "Every battle I've fought before today was for my country. This one is for my love," he declared. He placed the pistol back inside the trunk and went into the house.

Abby was standing in the kitchen near the wall mounted telephone holding the receiver to her ear. "I'm being connected to Higgins. They had to transfer me to his cell."

"Give me the phone," Brightpath said, holding out his hand.

Abby handed him the receiver and he stood patiently waiting. Finally, Higgins came on the line, "Agent Higgins."

"Higgins," he barked back, "this is Brightpath. I'm coming down there to help Sara, and I don't want you to interfere."

"What do you mean, help Sara?"

"She's been kidnapped by those guys that robbed the casino."

"How could you possibly know that?" Higgins asked.

"That's not important," Brightpath replied. "I'll be there in two hours. Just do us all a favor and let me do my job. If you do, she'll be okay, and I'll leave with no trouble. But if you try to stop me, your loved ones will be grieving tomorrow."

The phone went dead. Agent Higgins stared out the windshield of the helicopter. He had no idea that Sara was in danger, this changed the whole complexion of the case. Higgins pressed the transmit button on the radio after the shock wore off. "Commander, proceed with caution. I've just learned that our suspects may have a hostage."

"Copy," Moore replied.

● ● ● ● ●

As the search team made their way toward the inner parts of Bootlegger Cay, Commander Moore knew that it was time to get down to business. If a Skink Lizard farted within fifty meters of the man, he would surely smell it. Tom Moore operated at his peak in the jungle. That's how he knew that he made a major mistake when his next step felt different than the previous ones. Moore threw up his right arm and made a fist to signal the team to freeze in place. Jeb Cady buried a vine under the sandy soil and ran it underground to a nearby Oak tree. The vine ran up the tree and out across one of the limbs where it connected to a well-placed surprise. A burlap bag hanging overhead flopped upside down and dumped thirty Water Moccasin snakes down on the search team. The deadly reptiles hung in the tree for two days; they dropped out of the bag pissed off, hot and hungry.

The team members knew they couldn't dash away from the falling hazard because more booby traps may be waiting all around. All they could do was take out their razor-sharp knives and start slicing the slithering enemy. After the snakes were neutralized, Commander Moore slipped his knife back into the scabbard on his belt. "Damn, that was nasty." he remarked.

"Too nasty," Agent Blake called out from the rear of the formation.

Moore turned to laugh and saw that one of the snakes chomped into Blake's right pants leg refusing to let go. "Don't move," he shouted, "I'll get him."

Agent Blake replied calmly, "It's okay, he only got material." He pulled the snake's tail and stretched its full length for the others to see. "I think maybe it nipped the flesh, nothing serious," he said, cutting the reptile in half and tossing away the two pieces.

"Whoever these guys are, they're damned good," Commander Moore said. "We can't get them from the air or the ground. I think we better go back."

Blake agreed, "You might be right, boss. In this brush we may as well be blind. We can't see five feet ahead of us."

Commander Moore knew that this wasn't the work of your run-of-the-mill redneck. The aerial device that exploded in the trees demonstrated a tremendous knowledge of explosives, and the snake loaded trap exhibited a remarkable ability to use environmental resources to take out an enemy. The FBI search was good, but this job called for someone just as cunning and adept at moving through the unique landscape as the perpetrators.

The team retreated to the water. Captain Hawks lowered the helicopter to pick them up. Commander Moore and Agent Higgins discussed the situation on their way back to the airport. Moore recommended a call for military assistance, but Higgins quickly reminded him of the Posse Comitatus Act. That law passed in 1878 prohibits the use of military personnel within the U.S. borders for law enforcement purposes, unless authorization is granted by an act of Congress. That's why Higgins made it clear to Captain Hawks that he could only fly the helicopter while assigned to the mission.

Moore was frustrated. "Brother, I'm one of the best when it comes to dodging booby traps, but whoever constructed those things is much better than me."

Agent Higgins got the feeling that his search team was useless. He knew that Sara was in danger and Billy Brightpath could penetrate the island defenses to save her, but Higgins didn't know if he was strong enough to put aside his personal feelings and let Brightpath save her life. For the first time in his law enforcement career, Elroy Higgins was torn between doing his duty, and doing what he thought was right.

"Perhaps the solution to our problem is already on the way, gentlemen," Higgins said, dolefully "I just have to be man enough to let it happen."

A Matter of Honor

Brightpath and Abby took off for Everglades City. The ninety mile trip usually took about two hours, but when Brightpath hit the road, the accelerator hit the floor. Abby didn't say a word about the excessive speed, she knew it would do no good. She just pulled her seat belt tight and hung on for the ride. "You have no idea where Sara's being held," Abby said. "What are you going to do when we get there?"

Brightpath replied with purpose in his voice. "I bet Higgins knows. I'm going to find him first, then go from there."

"But he'll arrest you."

"Higgins is a good cop and smart man. He'll stay out of the way."

"I guess we'll see," Abby replied.

The search team gathered in Commander Moore's room for some afternoon poker, while Agent Higgins worked on daily reports in his short-term headquarters. He gave his agents another evening off so he could be alone to fight the coming emotional mêlée. His heart grappled with his mind over the situation with Sara, and each battle ended in a passionate draw. However, this time logic had an ally. Higgins had known for years that Sara was in love with Brightpath. It was a bitter pill to swallow, but it was time to put aside the feelings and do what needed to be done to save her life. Just when he got his head around the idea of Brightpath helping, a knock on the door broke his concentration. Higgins opened it and responded instinctively, "You're under arrest."

Abby shook a finger in Brightpath's face. "I told you what would happen, you dumbass!"

"It's not that easy," Brightpath told her. "He has to

actually take me, and from the look on his face, I'd say that he's not up to the task at the moment."

Higgins replied with a hint of dejection in his voice. "You're right. Come in, please."

"Don't do it Billy," Abby shouted, "it's a trap."

Agent Higgins took a step back. "No tricks, I promise. I need your help, but first I have a question. Are those grenades live?"

Brightpath looked down at the vest and teasingly said, "Not until I pull the pins."

"Okay, you trust me and I'll trust you," Higgins told him. "Please, give me a few minutes of your time."

When Brightpath and Abby entered the room, Higgins had an air of defeat about him. Brightpath picked up on it and tried to ease his sorrow. "Agent Higgins, I sense that you want to work out our differences. I also get the feeling that someone tried to ease your pain, but you rejected their compassion."

Higgins was amazed at how fast Brightpath tuned into his surroundings. That was apparently how he survived all of the hazardous missions during his military career. "Mr. Brightpath, I'm not going to play games here. Like I said before, I need your help, but I'm uncomfortable because of our mutual feelings for Sara."

"May I offer you some advice?" Brightpath asked.

"Of course."

"I carried my love for Sara over twenty years and it hurt me every day, but still I knew that it was the right thing. I knew that we would be together again someday, because I felt it in every part of me. Do you feel the same way? Do you know in your heart that your love for her is real, or are you just trying to keep your relationship alive because you're afraid to move on?

"If you can answer those questions honestly within

yourself, you might find that love is not what's causing these feeling. It may simply be fear."

Higgins stood quietly and listened as Brightpath spoke. He looked away in shame and subconsciously did an emotional self-evaluation.

Brightpath continued, "If your love for Sara is real, then you should let her go so she can be happy, but if your motivation is based in self-interest, you must let go for your own good. Only then can you move forward and give your passion to the one it is meant for.

"God in his infinite wisdom blessed us all with two of everything, two arms, two legs, two eyes and two ears. He also gave us two hearts, and somewhere in this world your true love carries your other heart."

Higgins turned away. His inevitable moment of truth was finally at hand. He walked to the window and pulled back the drapes just as a clap of thunder rumbled from a storm moving onshore. A tropical deluge fell on Everglades City, but the number of raindrops paled in comparison to the multitude of memories that raced through his mind. Higgins thought about why he'd held on through the years and realized that he still loved Sara, but he wasn't in love with her anymore. He looked back at Brightpath with watery eyes and exhaled a deep breath. "You're a good man, Mr. Brightpath, and I would be grateful if you would take care of her from now on."

Brightpath's chest swelled with pride, but it wasn't self-gratification that he displayed, it was a sign of respect for a good man and his ability to make the right choice. "I'll do my best," Brightpath proclaimed. "Now, let's get her out of this mess."

When the two men shook hands to make peace, Abby chimed in, "Not so damned fast. If he helps, what does he get?"

"He gets to save Sara," Higgins replied.

"No way," Abby fired back. "You're not offering him anything. Billy gets a walk on the Glades Corp thing. If not, we're out'a here."

Agent Higgins looked at Brightpath. "Who is this, your agent? I can't promise something like that. Those decisions are made by the Attorney General."

Brightpath smiled and said, "She's just trying to take care of me. I love her, but Abby can be pig-headed sometimes. If I can offer you one more bit of advice, I'd have to warn you not to piss her off. She's beautiful, but she can be mean when she has to."

Brightpath and Higgins both laughed. The tense atmosphere in the room eased with the moment of levity. When Abby started to speak-up to defend herself, Captain Hawks came in the door. She turned her attention to him. "Well, hello solider. Who are you?"

Hawks smiled and started to fire off one of his best one-liners, but he caught a glimpse of Brightpath in the corner of his eye. He quickly snapped to attention. Though a captain out ranks a sergeant major in the military chain of command, Hawks knew that Brightpath received the Congressional Medal of Honor and he was duty bound to salute the man on sight.

"As you were," Brightpath said. "It's good to see you again, Captain."

Hawks walked over and shook his hand. "You too, Tonto."

Abby's demeanor changed in a flash when she heard the name that Captain Hawks used to greet Brightpath. Thankfully, Brightpath looked over Hawks shoulder and saw Abby raise the back of her t-shirt. She slipped out the hunting knife hidden in her waistband at the small of her back. She started toward the Captain to stab his ass.

Brightpath pushed Captain Hawks aside and stepped between the two of them. "Hang on girl," he said with a laugh. "It's okay. He meant no harm."

Abby shot Hawks a wicked glare. "That shit ain't funny."

The Captain introduced himself. Though he'd been physically beaten by war and emotionally crippled by his ex-wife, when Rick Hawks turned on the charm he was still very appealing to the ladies. He flashed a smile and Abby responded in kind. For Captain Hawks the pain of being jilted faded slightly over time, but when he laid eyes on Abby, all of the sorrowful memories vanished forever. Her dark eyes mesmerized him and her long black hair accented the magnificent crimson skin tone of her face. Standing in front of Rick Hawks was the woman of his dreams, a sight that he envisioned in his mind many times, long before he ever knew that she actually existed.

While Abby and Captain Hawks unnecessarily tried to charm one another, Brightpath turned his attention back to Agent Higgins. "You give me the location where Sara is being held and I'll get her out. I'll even neutralize the guys holding her so you can make your arrest. Then, if you want to help me with the federal charge, you'll be doing it of your own free will."

Agent Higgins agreed to the deal. He shared all of the information that he had on the case and the two men laid out a plan of action. They examined a crude map of Bootlegger Cay and decided that Brightpath should infiltrate the island the following morning, but before he could begin the mission one final piece of the puzzle had to be in place.

Brightpath scribbled a name on a piece of paper and handed it to Higgins. "Find this guy and get him here.

Tell him that I need his help. If he gives you any static about coming, tell him that Brightpath needs to borrow a dollar."

Higgins looked confused. "What do you mean, barrow a dollar?"

"Just do it. If you say those words, he has to help. He has no choice."

"But, I have Tom Moore and his rescue team already here," Higgins said. "They can back you up. They're the best the FBI has."

"Moore, huh…," Brightpath repeated. "He's pretty good, but he never finished better than third in the Best Ranger competition. Get the guy I want, or I go alone. I'm going to get Sara out, even if you don't want my help, but you won't get to make your arrest."

Higgins looked at the name written on the paper. "This guy must be good."

Brightpath nodded his head. "He's the only one that I trust to back me up with something like this."

Agent Higgins put the note in his pocket and looked around the room for Captain Hawks. Both he and Abby had slipped out the door while Brightpath and Higgins talked. "Where could he have gotten off to so quickly?" Higgins asked.

Brightpath shook his head feigning disgust. "I've got a pretty good idea. Does he have a room nearby?"

"No, he's been bunking in an airport hangar. Says he don't want to leave his chopper alone at night."

Brightpath opened the door and looked out through the pouring rain toward the parking lot. He let out a loud whistle and Abby's head popped up in the back seat of an FBI sedan parked outside the door. Captain Hawks eased up alongside her with a smile on his face.

"I can't take her anywhere," Brightpath said, with lighthearted frustration.

Abby opened the car door and stepped out to button her blouse. "Who the hell are you whistling at? I ain't a damned horse."

"What happened to your thing with Austin Decker?"

"He was just a fun distraction for a little while."

Brightpath pulled a wad of cash from his pocket and handed it to Abby. "Will you try to harness your urges long enough to get us a room? We're going to stay here tonight."

Abby looked at Captain Hawks and smiled. "Oh yeah."

"On second thought, maybe you'd better make that two rooms," Brightpath suggested.

● ● ● ● ●

Agent Casey Reichmann worked at the computer trying to track down anything she could on the Sons of the New Confederacy. She possessed a true distain for racist groups that was unequalled. Casey's mother sat her down at the impressionable age of thirteen and had a long discussion with her about the family heritage. She told Casey that her grandfather, Hans Reichmann, came to the United States by way of Norway during World War II. Hans was a promising young violinist whose musical genius was well-known throughout Europe, but when he discovered what his father was doing for the war effort, Hans had to leave Germany forever.

One evening in the fall of 1943, Hans Reichmann put his violin case and a backpack into a small rowboat on the northeastern shore of Germany. He started his journey to America by crossing the dangerous waters of the North Sea that separated the Fatherland from the island nation of Great Britain. The trip was treacherous to say the least. The strong current and frigid winds that flow swiftly from the ice cold North Atlantic pushed against the little boat for most of the trip. Hans was at the point of total exhaustion after two days and nights of rowing, and just when he was about to give up and surrender his fate to the sea, lights came into view on a distant shoreline. Hans didn't see the lights as a sign of safety, he saw them as beacons of freedom for future descendants.

Sadly, Hans didn't make it to England that night. The tide pushed the boat in an easterly direction for the entire trip and he wound up in a Norwegian fishing village. Feeling that he was better off there than in his war-torn homeland, Hans worked the fishing docks in hopes of escaping Europe someday. He labored from sun up to sundown, then slumbered most nights in a cardboard box beneath a bridge. His diet consisted of the fish that no one would buy and the scraps of bread that a local baker couldn't sell. Hans Reichmann was determined to do whatever it took to escape the horrible shadow that his father cast on the family.

Casey's mother told her during their discussion that Reichmann wasn't actually the family name, it was Eichmann, and Hans' father was the monstrous Nazi Colonel, Adolf Eichmann; the architect of what became known throughout Germany as The Final Solution. When Hans discovered that his father was responsible for killing millions of Jews, he couldn't handle the guilt and he left Germany behind. Though he left a loving mother and younger sister, Hans knew that the only way he could escape his father's evil deeds would be to separate himself from his heritage forever.

After several months of eating garbage and sleeping in the bitter cold night air of Norway, Hans Reichmann finally saved enough money to book passage on a freighter to Nova Scotia. From there he took a perilous sixteen day hike through the wilds of Canada and eventually made his way into the United States by sneaking across the border near Niagara Falls.

Fate was good to Hans Reichmann and his timing couldn't have been better. The war ended at the same time he slipped across the border and immigrants were coming from Europe to America by the millions. It was easy for a man of his intelligence to fade into the multitude of foreigners flooding into the United States. Hans landed a busboy job in a Jersey Shore fine dining establishment where the owner overheard him playing the violin one night after closing. The man realized that Hans was wasting his talents cleaning tables and washing dishes, so the next evening he started working as a musician in the club orchestra.

A few of months later, Hans Reichmann was hired as a studio musician for CBS Radio in New York City. He was paid the staggering amount of one hundred and twenty dollars a week. Hans lived off half of his wages and used the rest to start his own musical production company in 1948 promoting the local jazz musicians.

Hans Reichmann made a fortune in the following years. All of the pieces fell into place for him and he was living the American dream. He established himself financially, married a good woman and became a father himself, but still the sins of the father haunted the son. Hans realized that good fortune came his way because he turned his back on the evil that was thrust upon him at a young age. He wanted to make sure that his chosen name would represent good forever, so Hans started an endowment program with his riches in 1957. He paid the college tuition for hundreds of less fortunate and minority students over the years until his death.

Knowing that her family fortune helped many of those less fortunate did nothing to appease Casey's pain, and she entered the field of law enforcement with the intent of stopping racism to the best of her abilities. Agent Reichmann saw the casino case as a chance to halt what she believed to be a gang of racist hooligans, and she wasn't going to rest until they were all behind bars.

● ● ● ● ●

Agent Higgins went back to his desk and got the wheels in motion to have the backup man in Everglades City as soon as possible. The walls unexpectedly shuttered and shouts filled the air outside the door. "Son-of-a-bitch," he heard Tom Moore bellow.

Higgins rushed outside and found Moore pacing the breezeway. "What's wrong, Commander?"

"That damned Blake. He sucked out a full house on the river to beat my nut flush."

Higgins wrinkled his brow. He never played poker before, but it was pretty obvious that what happened was bad. While Moore walked off the bad beat and explained everything to Higgins, Sonny Blake was at the poker table collecting the hundred dollar bounty from the other guys in the game.

"Sounds like an earth shattering event," Higgins joked. "But I need you to put away the games for a few minutes and come inside. There's been a change and we need to discuss what's going to happen tomorrow."

"Do we need Captain Hawks?" Moore asked.

"I think he's going to be busy for the remainder of the evening."

Moore followed Higgins into the room and they went over the details for infiltrating Bootlegger Cay. When he heard that Billy Brightpath was there and

101

going to be part of the mission, Moore lit up like Time Square. "Are you kidding me? He's actually here?"

During his military days, Moore heard stories of the Red Ghost, and Brightpath was a kind of superstar among the ranks. Moore also remembered competing against him in the Best Ranger contest, but he never had the opportunity to meet the man.

"Don't look so damned excited," Higgins said. "The man's a wanted criminal."

"Then why didn't you arrest him?"

"I was just about to explain that when you turned into Ralphy's little brother on Christmas morning. Now, if you'll calm down and listen, I'll fill you in on everything."

Higgins laid out the rescue plan and began to accept the fact that Billy Brightpath really wasn't such a bad guy after all. It suddenly seemed that everything in life was going in the right direction because he took Brightpath's advice to heart. The suspects would be in custody the following day, the case would be wrapped up, and Higgins was finally putting down the emotional baggage that he'd carried for so long.

When the briefing ended and Commander Moore left the room, Agent Reichmann's game day social call suddenly had its intended effect. Higgins felt good about the visit but for some reason he was torn again. However, this time it was more like a schoolboy trying to muster up enough courage to approach the cutest girl in class. His mouth got dry and Higgins couldn't work up enough spit to soften a saltine, but in his heart the old Elroy began to awaken after years of hibernation.

Higgins looked at the wall and knew that Casey was just on the other side. He paced the floor and tried to work up the nerve to go knock on her door, but he finally flopped back down in his desk chair and mumbled to himself, "All you have to do is, do it, damn man."

Caribbean Cookin'

The storm finding its way ashore was what southern folks like to call a freak of nature. It started an eight day trek when two thunderstorms bumped together off the coast of Belize. The meteorological combatants tussled for a while and then wound up joining forces before heading north. After percolating over the warm waters of the Caribbean Sea for five days, the storm started spewing sixty mile per hour winds and danced its way into the Gulf of Mexico. This was a most unusual occurrence for the month of January, and the National Hurricane Center in Miami found itself having to name the year's first tropical storm. Once it shot through the straights between the Yucatan Peninsula and the island nation of Cuba, Tropical Storm Alfalfa made a hard right hand turn and took dead aim at Everglades City.

A blinding rain fell and the howling winds blew through the trees on Bootlegger Cay. To make matters even worse, a storm surge pushed ashore and covered the entire island with eight inches of sea water. Sara spent the evening sitting on a tree limb hanging on for dear life, while the Sons of the New Confederacy splashing around in the floodwaters chasing money bags that the storm tried to wash out to sea.

While Sara and the boys suffered through the full brunt of the storm, the gang in Everglades City hunkered down in the motel to ride out the foul weather. Commander Moore and his team played poker all night, while Agent Higgins worked on the final details of the coming mission. Brightpath knew that he wasn't going to be able to sleep, so he tried to occupy his mind by reading his favorite book; The Old Man and the Sea. He still had the very same copy that White Feather gave him for his tenth birthday. Abby and

Captain Hawks decided to weather the storm together, and they created a little thunder and lightning of their own in the process. When Brightpath finished reading and tried to get some sleep, the rhythmic banging of the headboard from the room next door delayed his slumber for hours. About the same time the pleasure tempest came to a simultaneous conclusion in Abby's room, Tropical Storm Alfalfa blew inland and the weather took a turn for the better on the west coast of Florida. The rain stopped and the water receded on Bootlegger Cay. The wind lowered to a gentle breeze and Sara came down out of the tree.

Cletus T. ambled over with his head hanging and expressed a heartfelt apology. "I sure am sorry, ma'am. You alright?"

"Yes, I'm okay," Sara replied. "Soaked to the bone, but I'm good."

Cletus saw Junior and Bubba sloshing about picking up money bags, but Jeb Cady was nowhere in sight. Just when he started to let out a yell, Jeb stepped through the foliage coming back from the canal. "The boat's gone," he announced. "We got no way to get back."

"Infuckingcredible," Cletus T. shouted. "This whole thing has been just one disaster after another. I'm going home, anybody want to join me?"

Bubba sided with Cletus T., but Junior was still having serious reservations about not being able to swim. "I can't do it, boys. I might drown."

Cletus couldn't believe that Junior was still having a problem with leaving the island. "Look around, dude. The camp's washed away and our supplies are gone. If you stay here, you're goin'a die for sure."

Sara jumped in the discussion. "He's right. We all have to go back."

Jeb Cady pulled a pistol from his back pocket and pointed it at her. "You ain't going nowhere, woman."

"What are you doing, Jeb?" Junior yelled.

Jeb turned to his friends. "That's more money than I've ever saw in my life, and I damned sure ain't going to just walk off and leave it here on this island."

Cletus knew Jeb was serious. "This ain't right, Jeb. We all agreed from the start that nobody was going to get hurt. This lady ain't done a damned thing for you to be threatenin' her like that."

"If she makes it back, she'll tell everybody where we are," Jeb explained. "You boys can take some cash and go if you want, but me and the reporter are staying here."

Cletus T. couldn't believe the way things turned out. The robbery started as nothing more than a drunken stunt, but it turned into a federal piracy charge and now a hostage situation.

● ● ● ● ●

Agent Higgins worked frantically tracking down Brightpath's requested backup man. After accessing a top secret database and getting the needed information, he issued a nationwide bulletin and within minutes every law enforcement officer in America was looking for the guy. A soft knock on the door interrupted his work. Agent Reichmann opened the door and entered. She'd gathered all the information on each individual member of the Sons of the New Confederacy and brought it to Higgins. "Here's the info you asked for," she said, holding out a thick stack of paperwork.

Higgins came from behind his desk to take the papers and then walked into the adjacent kitchenette to pour a cup of coffee. "Anything new on Cletus T.

Walker?"

"No sir, just the drug charge."

"There's no way a bunch of dumbass rednecks pulled this job," Higgins insisted. "If they're all like the two we have in custody, I don't know how they tie their shoes without screwing it up."

Reichmann offered her opinion of the gang. "They may be rednecks, but they're not stupid. Maybe you're underestimating these guys. Either that or they are the luckiest bunch of sons-of-bitches in the world."

When Higgins turned to go back to his desk, Reichmann was standing in the doorway between the kitchen and the main room area. She put her left hip against the doorframe and grabbed the other side with her right hand to block his way.

"Agent Reichmann, there's a time and place for everything," Higgins said. "Playing around is out of the question at the moment. But that won't be the case when this thing is wrapped up," he added, with a sly grin. "You could stick around and help me out if you want."

Agent Reichmann stepped aside to let him pass. This was the first time that Higgins showed interest in anything other than work or football since she'd been assigned to the Miami office. Reichmann sent out a lot of playful signals over the last few months just to see if there was any attraction on Higgins part. On each occasion, her gestures were met with a businesslike response, but this time she saw a sparkle in his eye that was never there before.

Reichmann caught Higgins leaning close and taking a whiff of her perfume a couple of times during the evening. He even turned the TV monitor to a music channel so they could enjoy some good tunes while they worked. She had no idea what brought about this new attitude on his part, but Reichmann enjoyed the new Elroy Higgins. After all of the years of grief on both of their parts, it was starting to look as though fate stepped in and brought them together at just the right time.

The agents worked late into the night tracking down the requested support man, who was finally tracked down in New Orleans, Louisiana. Higgins spoke to him by phone a little after 11:00 PM, and the guy initially refused to join the mission. But once he heard that Brightpath needed to borrow a dollar, his attitude changed and the mystery man was eager to take part. He boarded a private airplane within an hour and was whisked off to Florida in the dead of night.

With the task complete and the hour growing late, Agent Higgins decided to call it quits until morning. He shut down his laptop and closed the lid, then asked Agent Reichmann if she would like to join him for a nightcap. She tactfully accepted and the two of them made small talk over cocktails for hours. Higgins was a little edgy at first and stumbled over his words a few times, but soon the conversation came easy and the company was just what they both needed.

● ● ● ● ●

When the sun came up the following morning the Ten Thousands Islands were in environmental recovery mode. Cletus T. and the boys got right down to business and had a serious discussion about which direction to take their little enterprise. Cletus T., Bubba and Junior were all ready to pack it in and go home, but Jeb Cady still had other plans. With Boo and Little Moe already in custody, and the rest of the gang ready to give up, Jeb knew that time was running out. However, he wasn't going to give up on the lucrative escapade as easily as the others.

"Alright, Cletus T., if you fella's want to go home, I ain't goin'a stop ya," Jeb said. "Ya'll can each take a bag of cash and go, but what you leave behind is mine."

Junior looked at Cletus through weary eyes. "I don't give a shit about the money. I'm tired, wet, and hungry. I just want to get the hell out'a here."

Bubba seconded the motion. "He can have the damn money. Let's go home."

Cletus T. walked over and extended a hand. "I hope there's no hard feelings, bro."

"I can't believe that you boys are giving up like this," Jeb declared. "When I get the rest of this money back home, I don't want you chumps coming around asking for a cut. Screw all of ya. You're dead to me."

"The lady goes with us," Cletus T. insisted.

"Nope, no way," Jeb replied. "We've all heard that chopper buzzing over the islands. The law will be here soon and I'm going to need a hostage."

Bubba jumped up from a fallen tree he was sitting on. "I say we put it to a vote."

Jeb snapped back, "Ain't goin'a be no damn vote. I'm not part of your group no more, remember. Now get your stuff together and I'll lead ya'll out'a here."

Jeb guided the group through the trap filled jungle to the eastern shore of the island. They knew that the water wasn't very deep most of the way back to the mainland, but there was still a few hazards that had to be considered. Cletus T. assumed that the storm sent most of the dangerous reptilians in search of higher ground during the night and the odds of being served up as Jurassic breakfast were greatly reduced. Junior put aside his fear of drowning once he realized there was nothing left to eat, and Bubba was just tired of the whole damned mess and wanted to get home. So with a bag of cash in one hand and a weapon in the other, the modern day rebels waded into the shallow water and headed for the Florida peninsula.

Jeb let Sara eat a Slim Jim found amongst campsite rubble, then he tied her to a tree and vanished into the jungle. The home court advantage definitely belonged to Jeb Cady. He grew up around the islands and spent many summers exploring them during his adolescent years. If he was going to have any chance at all of defeating the expertise of Billy Brightpath at the art of jungle warfare, it was going to take every bit of the knowledge and experience he had at his disposal. Jeb re-enforced Bootlegger Cay with even more traps and readied himself for the looming invasion.

● ● ● ● ●

Volunteers cleaned storm debris from the streets while power crews worked to restore electricity to the few parts of Everglades City that went dark during the night. Agent Higgins went to Commander Moore's room at eight o'clock sharp and knocked on the door. Sonny Blake opened it and Higgins saw the team still sitting around a poker table.

"What's up?" Blake asked.

"Tell your boss that it's time to go."

Blake looked at the morning sky and shouted over his shoulder, "Wow, we played all night, boys."

Commander Moore stepped around Blake and went out the door. "Not to worry, you guys are sitting this one out."

"Who's doing the search?"

"Billy Brightpath."

Blake was one of the military guys on the team, so

110

he too had heard stories about the Red Ghost. "Yeah right, and Santa Claus is his backup man."

While Higgins and Moore discussed the plan over breakfast, and Captain Hawks readied the chopper at the airport, Brightpath went through his customary pre-mission ritual on the shore of Lake Placid. Wearing just a pair of black fatigue pants and field boots, he prayed for guidance and readied himself for battle. Brightpath chanted to the spirits and marked his face with shoe polish as if applying war paint. He drew a thick black line below each eye that ran down his cheeks to the ridge of his muscular jaw. From the corner of his eyes a line ran straight back to each ears. The long black hair that grew unchecked for months was pulled back into a ponytail and tied in place with a leather string. Brightpath completed his spiritual preparations by making a black zigzag pattern across the full width of his forehead.

Now that the body and soul where ready for battle, the weaponry had to be applied. Brightpath slipped on the grenade loaded Kevlar vest and secured the zipper. He strapped the heirloom, panther bone hunting knife to his right thigh, then wrapped the trusty two holster gun belt around his waist. After pulling the slide back to ensure the readiness of each pistol he was ready for war.

Brightpath took a deep breath and looked to the sky. "Let's do this thing."

The tropical storm created something of a problem with getting the backup man to town. His flight had to be diverted to Port Charlotte, Florida, and he was transported from there to Everglades City by car. The land leg of the journey was going to push things back until the late morning hours, but Agent Higgins knew that the longer they waited, the more danger Sara faced.

After waiting over an hour, he started the mission without the backup man.

Brightpath dropped out of the helicopter into the water off Bootlegger Cay. Captain Hawks quickly turned the chopper around and headed back for Everglades City to ensure a quick delivery of the support personnel when he arrived. Brightpath made his way ashore and the foliage was so thick that he couldn't see more than a few feet into the brush. He hadn't experienced jungle like this since his early missions in the Amazon Rain Forest. Fifteen steps into the thicket, a bamboo shaft whipped up from the ground and Brightpath threw up a forearm to block the incoming threat. On the end of the shaft was a crudely made, ten inch long, razor sharp bamboo spike that would have penetrated his forehead had he not moved with the speed of a Cobra. This was obviously going to be a hazardous mission.

Moving through the jungle like a lion on the prowl, Brightpath didn't make a sound as he negotiated the untamed environment. The dark tree canopy overhead cast a daunting shadow on the island. The dense brush was challenging to say the least. With no pre-mission reconnaissance information available on the possible location of Sara, and no topographical map of the island terrain, Brightpath moved practically blind through the wild surroundings.

Agent Higgins setup a mission control center in the aircraft hangar at the airport. The center was equipped with a communications console for contact with all of the operatives, a radar screen to observe the helicopter and a satellite map of the Ten Thousand Islands that covered a large portion of one wall. A quick check of the communications link between the control center, the chopper, and Brightpath went well, but once that was complete an uneasy silence filled the cavernous building.

Agent Reichmann assisted with manning the post. She sat at the radio controls while Higgins watched the helicopter approach on the radar screen. A true spark ignited between the two of them during their late night encounter, but both were trying hard to keep things on a professional level so they could deal with the mission at hand. That was something easier said than done. The awkward silence ultimately got to Higgins. He had to say something to ease the tension. "Agent Reichmann, thank you for last night. I enjoyed your company very much. You did more for my self-esteem than the whole damned caravan of shrinks that I've talked to over the years."

Reichmann never took her eyes off the console. "It was nice," she replied.

A black SUV with tinted windows pulled in through the massive open hangar doors and stopped. One of the rear doors opened and a man stepped out wearing blue jeans, a Welcome to New Orleans t-shirt and brown leather loafers with no socks. He was a well-built guy of average height and weight, but his face displayed the scars of many battles. In his left hand he carried a trombone case covered with tattered black leather.

Higgins came from behind the console and walked around to greet the man, just as Captain Hawks lowered the helicopter outside the hangar doors and landed. Abby was riding shotgun in the co-pilot seat and couldn't believe her eyes when she looked inside the hanger. She snatched the sidearm from the Captain's gun belt and jumped out of the chopper to dash into the hangar.

"What the fuck is he doing here?" Abby shouted. She pointed the pistol at the man's face. He dropped the trombone case and reached for the sky with both hands.

"Brightpath asked for him," Higgins told her.

"That's bullshit. Billy would never ask for this guy. He almost killed Sara."

Major Weldon Sparks didn't move a muscle, looking down the business end of the forty-five caliber pistol pointed at his nose. The hole at the end of the barrel looked big enough to stick his head in. "You shoot me and this mission is over," he said.

"The Sergeant Major asked for me because he wants to make sure that the job is done right. He must have a vested interest in this thing. How about you put away the weapon and someone tell me what's going on here?"

"No way, asshole" Abby said. "I'm going to kill you where you stand."

By this time, Captain Hawks joined the party. He could tell by the expression on her face that Abby was going to kill Major Sparks. She had the same cold look in her eyes that Michael Corleone displayed when Sal Tessio begged for his life.

"Wait, I have an idea," Hawks said. He went to the radio console and picking up the microphone. "Base to Brightpath."

The console speaker cracked. "Brightpath, go."

"We have your backup man here, but Abby wants to kill him."

"Can she hear me?"

"Yes, we all can," Captain Hawks replied.

Brightpath had to stop the search so he wouldn't be distracted by the conversation. "Abby, what are you doing?"

"I'm going to kill this worthless piece of shit," she shouted. "Why would you have him brought here after what he did?"

"I need him, that's why. I have to make sure that Sara gets out of here alive if I go down, and he's the only one that has the ability to do that."

Abby couldn't believe his reasoning. "But he's already tried to kill her once. And he would have killed me too, if I hadn't shot him on the porch that night."

Major Sparks rubbed the scare running across his forehead. "Yeah, and I ain't forgot that shit either."

The speaker blared, "Shut up, Sparks. She'll kill you."

Agent Higgins looked at Abby. "If you will excuse us ma'am, we're going to step outside and let you folks work this out amongst yourselves." He turned back to Agent Reichmann. "Let's go."

"Hang on a minute," the Major begged. "You're the law. You can't leave me here with this crazy woman pointing a gun at my face."

Higgins didn't know that Weldon Sparks was the one that shot Sara. He paused as he walked by the Major on the way out the door. "If I had known that you were the one who shot Sara, I would have had you killed in New Orleans," he whispered, than continued on his way out of the hangar.

Brightpath couldn't believe that he had to stop everything and deal with Abby right in the middle of the mission. He was in danger, and only God knew if Sara was okay, but none of that mattered to Abby because she was pissed off. Brightpath knew that he had to do something or Major Sparks would be a dead man.

"Abby, he has to help," Brightpath said. "I sent him a coded message and he has no choice. Hasn't he proven that by being here?"

Abby tightened her finger on the trigger. "You don't need him, Billy. You can save Sara without this guy."

Brightpath looked up to the heavens and shook his head in frustration. "Okay, if you're going to kill him, go ahead and do it. I can't stop you from here. But, I do need his help, and I can't get it if he's dead."

Abby heard the desperation in his voice. She considered his plea and the deadly glare slowly faded from her eyes. She took her finger off of the trigger. "Can I kill him when you guys are finished?"

"We'll discuss that later," Brightpath said, "but for now, just trust me."

Abby lowered the weapon and Captain Hawks took it from her hand. "Were you really going to shoot the guy?"

"Bet your ass, I was," Abby replied.

"She already has once," Major Sparks announced, lowering his hands.

Hawks chuckled. "Damn, woman, I'd hate to piss you off."

Abby stormed out of the hangar as the FBI Agents came back inside. Sparks picked up his trombone case and asked Agent Higgins where he could ready himself for the mission. Higgins escorted him to a restroom and asked about the case, "What's inside?"

Major Sparks opened the top and proudly displayed an M-110 SASS, 7.62 millimeter, sniper rifle. "My favorite instrument," he replied with a villainous smile.

●　●　●　●　●

While Agent Reichmann wired Major Sparks with a hands free radio system, Agent Higgins spoke to the federal attorney general on a telephone, and Captain Hawks tried to cool Abby down outside the hangar.

After a hasty mission briefing for the Major, he and

116

Captain Hawks got in the chopper and took off. Hawks flew the helicopter a hundred feet above the surface and spotted three men wading in the water about half way out to Bootlegger Cay. At the same time, Cletus T. saw the chopper approaching. He took a deep breath and submerging himself in an attempt to hide.

Major Sparks peered through his rifle scope and saw Cletus go under. "Didn't Agent Higgins say that the loot was taken from the casino in blue canvas bags?"

"That's correct," Hawks said.

"Well, these guys are toting big blue bags. They're also carrying weapons."

Captain Hawks hovered the chopper a safe distance away from the band of revolutionaries and informed the command center of the sighting. Agent Higgins ordered him to stay in visual contact with the suspects until the Coast Guard arrived to pick them up. Cletus T. popped back up through the surface and gasped for air, just as Junior aimed a shotgun and fired at the helicopter. The buckshot fell harmlessly into the water and never got close to the chopper, but the aggressive act was all that Major Sparks needed to have a little fun. A smile came to his face. Sparks pulled the trigger on his rifle and Cletus T.s' money bag ripped open. All of the cash poured out and covered the surface around the suspects with a blanket of hundred dollar bills.

"Shit," Major Sparks bellowed. "I must have knocked the scope out of alignment when I dropped the case."

Bubba yelled, "Their shootin' at us." He dropped the pistol from one hand and let go of the money bag in the other, then raised both hands in the air and froze in place.

Junior carelessly set his money bag adrift when he

had to use both hands to fire the shotgun, but he too dropped his weapon and surrendered after hearing the return gunfire from the helicopter.

Cletus T. wasn't about to surrender so easily. He let the money bag go when it ripped open and submerged himself again. When he dropped into the chest deep water a second time, Cletus found himself nose to nose with an eight hundred pound, twelve foot long, North American bull crocodile. He shot back up through the surface like a submarine launched ballistic missile and shouted, "Crocodile, crocodile, crocodile." He kicked and pulled at the water like Michael Phelps after a couple tokes off a crack pipe.

Captain Hawks moved the helicopter closer once the suspects were unarmed. Major Sparks lowered his rifle to turn the adjustments knobs on the scope. When he returned the weapon to the shoulder ready position, the hungry crocodile surfaced and the Major targeted the creature. With a keen eye and a steady hand, he fired and hit the ravenous beast square in the back. "Dammit, my shots are high and to the right. I was aiming for its head."

The bullet lodged in the crocodile's thick hide and stung just enough to send the creature in search of a more trouble-free brunch. Thankfully, the beast went one way and Cletus T. went the other.

While Bubba and Junior huddled together with their hands in the air, Cletus T. kept swimming with amazing resolve. Captain Hawks flew a circle over the yielding insurgents until a Coast Guard boat eased up beside them. The boys climbed onboard to surrender without resistance. Once they were onboard, Hawks did a quick search of the vicinity and found nothing but sea water and tiny islands.

"Hawks to base."

"This is base, what you got, Captain."

"Two of your suspects are aboard the CG cutter, but a third one vanished."

"What do you mean, vanished?"

"He's just gone, sir. That's all I can tell you."

Out'a the Bag

Agent Reichmann stayed on the phone with the Coast Guard dispatcher until the captain onboard the boat confirmed the identity of the men plucked from the sea. She ended the call and turned to Higgins. "It looks like this thing is coming together very nicely. Four down, two to go."

Higgins marked the spot on the map where the two men were apprehended. He wondered how Cletus T. could have possibly slipped away so easily. "The man's amazing," he remarked. "How could he have possibly vanished into thin air?"

Reichmann came to the map and stood beside him. Higgins leaned in her direction and breathed in the fragrance. Agent Reichmann took the marker from his hand and drew a circle with a one mile radius around the spot. "There are more than thirty islands in the area," she said. "He had to swim to one of them."

Higgins turned away from the map and focused his attention on Reichmann. "What's up with your cold response a few minutes ago? I thought you enjoyed our little talk last night."

"We're working," Agent Reichmann replied. "You never know when one of the others might walk in."

Higgins moved closer and glared at her lips. "I sent the others back to Miami this morning."

Reichmann slipped off her glasses and their eyes locked. "Why now?" she asked softly. "I've been trying to get your attention for a long time."

"I was an emotional wreck until last night," Higgins replied. "You touched a part of me that's been out of reach for years. It felt great."

Higgins surprised her with his affectionate conduct. His normal professional work ethic seemed to be somewhere else. They both filled with desire. Their lips were on the verge of touching when her inner purpose invaded the moment. "We can't do this," Reichmann insisted. Her attitude changed in the blink of an eye. "I want to catch these racist bastards and lock them up forever."

Higgins took a step back. "I'm not so sure that these guys are racist."

"What do you mean?"

"We haven't heard anything from them to lead us to that conclusion. I think the Confederate flag thing was just a misguided sign of their frustrations."

Higgins went on to explain that not one of those in custody made a single derogatory comment about skin color, nationality, religion, sexual orientation, or even gender. He came to the conclusion that the Sons of the New Confederacy was exactly what they appeared to be, a group of backcountry, good ole boys, that pulled off the first successful act of piracy in U.S. coastal waters in over a hundred years. But there was a more pressing problem that needed to be addressed. Higgins pointed to one of the chairs near the communications console. "Have a seat, Casey."

Higgins never called Agent Reichmann by her first name. She didn't know what to expect, especially after his bold move by the map. "I know about your great-grandfather," he told her.

Agent Reichmann lowered her head and looked away. "How long have you known?"

"I knew it long before you ever came to Miami. The Bureau found out everything during your pre-employment background check. We're very good at what we do."

Reichmann began to cry. Tears dripped down from her eyes onto her skirt.

121

Higgins continued, "If I might make a suggestion, don't let something bad that happened three generations ago be the driving force in your life. If you want a family example to live by, I think you should look to your grandfather, not his father. Did you know that three of the young people your grandfather put through college went on to become Congressmen? Another became Governor of Delaware and a fifth is currently serving as a member of the U.S. Supreme Court. Those are just a few examples of the tremendous good that came out of his work. There are countless others that I can point out if you want me to continue."

Agent Reichmann looked up at Higgins and wiped the tears from her eyes. The left corner of her mouth turned up slightly to make half a smile and she sniffled. "Thank you for understanding. It's obvious that it doesn't matter professionally, how about personally?"

Higgins gently caressed her left cheek. He looked into her eyes and smiled. "You're a magnificent person, Casey. It took an amazing woman to penetrate the emotional armor that I've been wearing all these years, and you're the one that did it."

Reichmann rose to her feet and they wrapped their arms around each other. When their lips met, Higgins recaptured the wholesome pleasures of holding a good woman in his arms. The emotional fears vanished and his long suppressed passion came back to life.

For Casey Reichmann the experience was even more fulfilling than she imagined. She made a true connection with a real man. It was nothing like the shallow relationships that she experienced in the past. This was thrilling and powerful, and most importantly, Higgins was man enough to lift the weight of the world off her shoulders. The fears of a little girl hiding a horrible secret were gone forever. Casey was at peace.

The horrors that Hans Reichmann fought so hard to distance the family from were at last a thing of the past for his lone surviving descendant.

The console speaker sounded, "Brightpath to base,"

Higgins backed away from her embrace and straightened his necktie. He cleared his throat and picked up the microphone. "This is base, go."

"How far out is my backup? I'm in some heavy jungle and its booby trapped to the max. I want to make sure that Sparks is going to take over if something goes wrong."

Agent Higgins called the chopper. Brightpath listened as Hawks confirmed that he would be dropping Major Sparks near Bootlegger Cay in one minute.

"I copy," Brightpath said. "Sparks, are you hot?"

Major Sparks instinctively referred to Brightpath by his military code name. "10-4, Ghost. What's up?"

"I'm leaving markers along the way so you can move quickly and catch up. Don't deviate from the trail, if you do you're dead. This place has more traps than Achmed's palace." Brightpath said, referring to a terrorist camp that the two of them infiltrated years earlier.

"Man, that job was a bitch," Sparks remarked. "But we busted up that little party forever. Poor old Achmed hasn't been seen since."

"And he never will be," Brightpath added.

Back in the com-center, Agent Reichmann pulled the bottom of her skirt with both hands to get the wrinkles out, while Agent Higgins tugged his shirt cuffs and straighten his jacket. The brief dialogue between the two warriors brought things back into perspective and it was time to get back to work.

● ● ● ● ●

Captain Hawks lowered the chopper off Bootlegger Cay in the same place where he deployed Brightpath. Major Sparks hopped out the portside hatch without saying a word. He dropped into the water holding the rifle overhead with both hands and quickly waded ashore. Sparks spotted a piece of orange tape attached to a palm tree at the edge of the island and knew that it was one of the markers Brightpath told him about. The marker made it easy for Major Sparks to see where the plants were parted and his colleague entered the jungle, so he plucked the tape off the tree and disappeared into the greenery.

Brightpath continued to blaze a trail ahead of Sparks, dodging manmade hazards along the way. Agent Higgins informed them by radio that four suspects were now in custody, and a fifth was last seen swimming away from island. Hearing that only one adversary remained on the island, Brightpath briefly let his guard down, and that turned out to be a terrible mistake. When he came to an easily detectible trap, Brightpath maneuvered around the obstacle and tripped a snare hidden in the brush. This released a sharp bamboo spear that sliced deep into his right arm. He stumbled to the left and fell victim to the real trap the decoy directed him toward.

When the soil softened under his feet, Brightpath experienced what's known in the South as an *igno-second*; that fraction of a second when your mind tells your body that you screwed up, but there ain't a damned thing you can do about it. He fell into what appeared to be the shallow remnants of the tropical storm, but to his surprise the water was much deeper than it looked. Jeb Cady dug the pit three feet deep and covered the bottom with the sharpened bamboo spikes.

The spikes were intended to penetrate the torso of any poor soul that happened to stumble into the pit, but the flood waters from the storm washed them out and left the hole filled with only muddy water. Unfortunately, a lazy old gator happened along earlier that morning and discovered the inviting pool. It was the perfect lounging environment for a prehistoric beast trying to evade the South Florida heat, so the creature decided to make full use of the facility.

Brightpath dropped into the pit and landed squarely on top of the sleeping alligator. This scared the hell out of both of them and the gator instinctively thrashed. Brightpath knew right away what happened. He reached for the knife strapped to his leg as he descended in the water. The alligator chomped into his thigh, sinking its teeth all the way to the bone. The intense pain made Brightpath drop the knife and it fluttered away until it found the bottom of the pit. He quickly pulled one of the pistols from his gun belt and jammed the end of the barrel firmly between the monster's eyes. When Brightpath pulled the trigger, the alligator let loose its crushing bite and turned belly up, then floated to the surface deader than Julius Caesar.

Brightpath rose up through the murky surface and pushed the dead gator aside. He made his way to the edge of the pit and crawled out with the pistol still in hand, then stood at the water's edge and looked down at the remains of the reptile. "Thankfully, Grandpa gave me something for just such an occasion." He unzipped his bulletproof vest and reached for the spirit bag but it wasn't there.

Blood gushed from the torn Femoral artery in his leg. Brightpath never faced serious injury without the spirit bag, so he pressed the transmit button on the radio to inform the com-center of his dilemma. "Brightpath to base," he called out, but there was no answer. The water flooded the radio and shorted out the inner electronics. His contact with the outside world was as dead as the lifeless gator floating in the pit.

Brightpath opened the cargo pocket dangling from his shredded pants leg and pulled out a Kotex. He pressed it against the wounds and secured the pad in place with a length of medical tape from the survival kit in a vest pocket. "My bag. Dear God, I need my bag."

● ● ● ● ●

Major Sparks shinned up a tree to overlooking the vegetation in hopes of making visual contact with Billy Brightpath. Looking through the rifle scope and moving it slowly right to left, he spotted a rustling in the jungle about sixty yards ahead. Brightpath popped his head up through the brush and Major Sparks smiled. He took a deep breath, exhaled slowly, paused and then squeezed off a shot from his rifle.

The bullet went over Brightpath's head and hit a palm tree to his right. He dropped to the ground and pressed the button on his dead radio again. "Someone's shooting at me. Do you read me, Sparks? Someone's shooting."

Major Sparks turned the adjustment knob on the side of the scope and peered through the eyepiece again. He sat absolutely still in hopes that Brightpath would show himself a second time. "Just one more time, red man, that's all I need. Pop that noggin up and let me do my magic."

Sara heard the gunshot and took the cellphone from her pocket. She pressed a speed dial button and the phone on Brightpath's hip buzzed. "Thank God for Samsung technology," he said, looking at the display.

"Sara, are you okay?"

"Yes, Billy, I'm hiding in the forest. I got away from the guy holding me, but I'm still on the island. Please, come quick."

"I'm here sweetheart, but I've been injured. I'm bleeding pretty bad and getting weak. I don't know how much farther I can go."

Sara knew that Brightpath wouldn't stop until he was physically unable to take another step. Still, she tried to convince him to do otherwise. "Stop, Billy. Stop where you are and rest, slow your heart rate. If you don't you might die."

Brightpath pressed on in his weakened state until he reached the clearing where the campsite had been. He still had the phone pressed to his ear and looked around for Sara. "I made it, baby. I found the camp. Where are you?"

Sara came out of hiding and started back to the camp. Jeb Cady dropped down from a tree and pointed his pistol at her face. "He's here, Billy," Sara shrieked, and the phone went dead.

Brightpath was physically spent. His mind filled with the many times that he defeated death and the thought of an alligator killing him seemed ironic. His vision faded to black and he used the meager remains of his rapidly fleeting strength to stand tall and shout with a booming voice, "Sara…"

Just as Brightpath rose and called out, Major Sparks popped up in the chest high vegetation behind him. Sara and Jeb stepped into the clearing and watched as the Major took aim and fired. Major Sparks responded with delight. "Sweet," he said, kissing the rifle stock.

Sara couldn't believe her eyes when she saw Brightpath go down to the wet ground. She dropped to her knees and screamed, "You cowardly bastard, you shot him in the back."

Silence Ain't Always Golden

Cletus T. waded along in the waist deep water about a mile from the mainland pondering his circumstances. He didn't have a dollar to his name, he pawned his pickup truck to finance the heist, and even lost his job in the process. Needless to say, things didn't turn out quite the way he expected.

A nice retired couple soon came along in their new thirty-five foot cabin cruiser and plucked Cletus T. from the sea. He wove an exciting tale about how he'd capsized his boat in the Gulf of Mexico the day before, spending a death defying night clinging to the hull while sharks circled in the waters all around. The couple got so caught up in the tale that they forgot to ask Cletus where he wanted to be taken ashore, so he just kept right on talking until they all disembarked in Marco Island.

The kind couple took pity on the poor shipwreck victim and insisted that he join them for a meal. At the very same time Cletus T. cut into a prime rib steak at the Marco Island Yacht Club, Agent Higgins started sweating bullets back in Everglades City. He jumped up from his chair behind the communications console and walked over to the open hangar doors. Higgins looked out at Chokoloskee Bay and mumbled, "Something's not right. I can feel it."

Agent Reichmann watched him from behind the console. She saw the worried look on his face and wished she could do something to help.

Higgins paced back and forth like an expectant father in a maternity ward. Almost an hour had passed since he last heard from his two operatives and Higgins was getting antsy. "Agent Reichmann, call Brightpath on the radio."

Reichmann leaned forward in her chair to press the transmit button on the console. "Base to Brightpath," she called out. Reichmann repeated the call several times but each went unanswered.

Agent Higgins rushed back to the radio and called out to Major Sparks. "Leave me alone," Sparks yelled. "I've got a situation here."

Higgins slammed his fist down on the console and shouted into the microphone. "Sparks…, Sparks…, answer me, damn you."

Agent Higgins called Captain Hawks back to the airport and then turned to Agent Reichmann. "Call the motel. Get Commander Moore and his team over here. I have to get them out there ASAP."

Reichmann made the call and watched Higgins fidget around like a cat in a dog pound. After speaking to Commander Moore, she asked Higgins why he was so worried.

"I have a bad feeling about this," he told her. "I know the history between these two guys and it's possible that something has gone wrong."

"What are you talking about?"

Higgins told Reichmann about the Glades Sugar Corporation case, and how Sara was almost killed by Major Sparks. He also told her about Brightpath and Sara's personal relationship. "If I could kick my own ass, I would do it," he said. "I should have never brought Sparks in on this thing."

After hearing that Sara and Brightpath were lovers, and that Sparks almost killed her, Agent Reichmann asked a very thought-provoking question. "Do you think maybe Brightpath had us bring Sparks here so he could kill him?"

Higgins considered the query for a second. "I hope not, but I really don't think he wants to kill the man. I know his capabilities. If he wanted the Major dead, we would've never found him alive."

Higgins reached under the console and picked up his briefcase. He opened it and took out a three inch thick file, then tossed it on the console in front of Agent Reichmann. "That's the Department Of Defense file on Mr. Brightpath. I read it last night and couldn't believe what I saw. He's capable of doing things that you and I can't even imagine.

"If you take what you can read in those pages and fill in the blacked out parts, the conclusion you draw is some scary stuff. Thankfully, he's on our side."

Reichmann opened the file and scanned the pages. "What does this have to do with Sparks?"

"Checkout the mission briefs starting back about twelve years ago," Higgins said. "Brightpath's backup man on all of those assignments was Weldon Sparks.

"I did a background check on the Major after his arrival and found some very disturbing facts. He was court marshaled two years ago and forced out of the Army for emotional reasons. Sparks has no record of steady employment since his discharge, but somehow he's made enough money to open three bank accounts. Each one has a balance of almost a million dollars."

Agent Reichmann looked through the document as she listened and got even more confused. "What's your point here? How does the Major's net worth have anything to do with this?"

Higgins leaned back in his chair. "Look at what these two men have done in the past. Now ask yourself a question, if Sparks has those talents and he's making massive amounts of money without being employed, just how do you think he's doing it?"

"Oh no…, he's a hit man," Reichmann said.

The severity of the situation hit Higgins like a

hammer right between the eyes. He acted on Brightpath's request without doing a proper background check on Sparks, and now it might come back to bite both of them in the ass.

Captain Hawks interrupted the conversation when he swooped the helicopter down and landed outside the hangar doors. He stepped out of the aircraft and Abby rushed to greet him with a kiss and a cold bottle of water. The drink was a welcomed gesture for the weary pilot. He'd been flying for hours and the Florida heat was starting to take its toll. The temperature inside the cockpit reached the three digit mark and the humidity was so thick you could cut it with a chainsaw. The Captain's flight suit was soaked with sweat from top to bottom. He turned up the bottle of water and killed it in three big gulps, then wiped his mouth with a sleeve and said one word, "Beer."

Abby laughed. "Okay, honey. I'll get you a sandwich too." She walked off toward the airport lounge.

The Captain took off his flight helmet and strolled into the hangar. Agent Higgins looked up and Hawks saw the anguish in his eyes. "What's the word, chief?"

"There's been no word," Higgins told him. "That's the problem. Moore is on the way over with his guys. I'll brief you all at once."

By the time the team gathered in the hangar, Abby returned with lunch for Captain Hawks. When Higgins explained the problem and changed the mission status from suspect search to possible rescue, Abby went off like a distressed postal worker. "You got'a be shitting me," she shouted. "How could you send Sparks out there without knowing who you're dealing with?"

Silence filled the hangar. Higgins looked at Captain Hawks. "Dude, don't look to me for help," Hawks told him. "I've been to bed with her. If she fights like she makes love, you're ass in trouble."

Agent Higgins walked over to Abby and tried to calm her. He put a hand on her shoulder for comfort. "I'm sorry, ma'am. I had no idea that Major Sparks was so dangerous. I'm going to do all that I can to make sure your cousin is okay."

Abby looked Higgins in the eye and he couldn't help admiring the way her jet black hair accented the dark brown eyes. It pained him to cause distress to such a beautiful woman, but the trepidation quickly vanished with the sting sensation near his groin. Abby eased her knife out while enticing him with her glare. She pierced the front of his pants near the zipper and pressed the tip of the knife blade against his lower abdomen. "Mr. Higgins, I accept your apology," she said coldly. "But if either Billy or Sara gets hurt, I'm going to cut your balls off and throw them in the bay."

Muffled snickers filled the air and Higgins heard a whisper from one of the team members. "Damn, she's hot when she's pissed."

"She's hot, period," another hushed voice said.

Captain Hawks wrapped his hand around her wrist. "Calm down, girl. He's just doing his duty."

Abby eased the knife away and slid it back into her waistband. "Well, he's doing a horrible fucking job. Any idiot could see that Sparks is trouble, but not this jerk-off, he didn't see a damned thing."

Captain Hawks walked Abby outside and convinced her to go to the lounge and wait there. He promised to let her know what was happening on Bootlegger Cay as soon as he got there, and assured her that Brightpath could handle any trouble that Major Sparks might stir up. Abby knew that Brightpath was the best in the world at his chosen profession, but her instincts just

133

wouldn't let her rest. "Let me go with you, Rick. I'll just sit quiet and ride along, like I did this morning. I promise."

"That may be hard to arrange. You just threatened to de-nut the guy that's in charge of this whole operation."

Abby put on her best pouty face, "Please..."

Captain Hawks smiled. "Damn, girl, you've got my number for sure. I'll see what I can do."

Abby went inside the lounge when Captain Hawks went back to the hanger. He asked Higgins if she could ride along on the next flight. Higgins shot up from his chair and leaned over the top of the communications console. He shook his finger like Bill Clinton telling the world that he didn't have sexual relations with that woman. "If you put that crazy woman in that chopper, I'm going to relieve you of duty and get me another pilot."

Higgins could see the disappointment in his face. He ordered Captain Hawks to stay in the hangar until it was time to lift off again. He didn't trust the Captain one bit when it came to Abby, because he had experienced firsthand how she can distract a man with her beauty.

● ● ● ● ●

Cletus T. Walker finished his gourmet meal, then strolled out of the yacht club like a member. He hiked along South Collier Boulevard and hoped his ride would show up soon, because Marco Island isn't your run-of-the-mill Florida town. The locals are what most refer to as privileged, so the site of a stranger walking along the highway brought a few curious looks from those speeding by in their European luxury sedans.

Cletus soon found himself surrounded by three

134

police cars and six of the city's finest employees. The officers were all built like NFL linemen. When they stepped out of their cruisers a massive shadow covered the roadside. It looked like a solar eclipse easing down the street in his direction as they approached in a tactical formation. Cletus T. kept his cool throughout the frightening encounter and calmly repeated the same disastrous seafaring story told to the elderly couple. He assured the officers that he was on the way out of their inviting little town and that his sister was on the way to pick him up.

The police officers on Marco Island have a sworn duty to ensure the safety and security of the overtaxed citizenry, so it came as no surprise to Cletus T. when one of them offered him transportation off the island. The officer opened the rear door of the cruiser and asked him to have a seat, but Cletus got suspicious and tried to sidestep the invitation.

"Naw, that's alright," he said, backing away. "I'll just walk."

"Sorry, sir, but I can't let that happen," the gigantic cop replied firmly.

Cletus T. looked out the corner of his eye and saw another officer maneuver around behind him. His butt puckered and he broke out in an instant flop-sweat. Cletus thought for sure that he was going to jail. Then suddenly, the distinct sound of a Volkswagen horn beeped twice and interrupted his foreboding thoughts.

"There she is, officers," Cletus T. said, pointing at the purple VW Beetle coming in their direction. "That's my sister, right yonder."

Cletus called Scarlett Wilkes from a yacht club lobby before sitting down to have lunch. He convinced her to come pick him up. Scarlett wasn't too happy about having to make the forty minute drive while

General Hospital was on, but she still had a soft spot in her heart for him and agreed to pass on her favorite soap opera.

Scarlett came to a stop behind one of the police cruisers on the side of the road. She got out of the car and walked toward Cletus T. One of the officers stopped her. "Do you know this man?" he asked, pointing at Cletus.

Cletus T. overheard the question and quickly called out, "Hey sis, thanks for coming to pick me up."

Scarlett knew that something fishy was going down, so she confirmed his false story. The officer harbored suspicions and demanded that she present some form of identification. Scarlett gave him her driver's license. The officer instructed her and Cletus T. to have a seat in the car and wait. She knew that the cops were doing a warrant check. Scarlett looked at Cletus T. "Well, are they going to find anything on you?"

Cletus laughed. "No way, I told them my name is Beavis Wilkes."

Her face turned whiter than a flounder's belly. "Oh, shit."

"What's wrong, girl?"

"I have an uncle in Daytona named Beavis. He's wanted on a grand larceny charge."

"Unfuckingbelievable," Cletus T. mumbled. "Of all the names that I could pick out of thin air, I had to pick one that matched a wanted felon."

Scarlett had no idea that Cletus was the mastermind behind the casino robbery, but while they sat cramped together in the sweltering little car, he filled her in on the whole story. She had no idea that her brother was in jail, or that he'd taken part in the heist. "I should turn your sorry ass over to the law right now," she shouted. "I can't believe that I'm going to be arrested for aiding a fugitive."

Cletus T. looked out at the traffic zipping by and considered making a dash for freedom, but he knew that the officers would surely chase him down and make him regret it. "No need in sweatin' it now," he said. "Let's just hope for the best and see what happens." He turned back to Scarlett and flashed his pearly whites. "You wouldn't happen to have a beer in the car, would ya?"

"A beer?" she screamed. "We're in this damn mess and all you can think about is a beer? That's how you live your whole damned life. You don't take anything seriously."

Cletus T. pointed out the windshield at the colossal cop approaching. "It looks like we're about to hear the verdict."

Scarlett rolled down the driver side window and the officer handed back her license. He leaned down to look at Cletus T. and asked, "Mr. Wilkes, what's your D.O.B.?"

Cletus T. responded with his actual date of birth. He knew that if the officer discovered the warrant for Scarlett's uncle, he would surely be too young to fit the age on the warrant. The officer stared at Cletus for a moment and then apologized for intruding on their day.

Scarlett started the car and pulled into traffic. She tried not to inflame the situation, but before she got the purple bug in third gear, Scarlett let loose. "You no good son-of-a-bitch, if you had any desire to better yourself, you would've straightened up before Sharon left you. Instead, you live your life like a twelve year old boy."

Cletus T. shrugged his shoulders. "I am what I am, pretty girl, and I reckon that's all I'll ever be."

Another Hero

The situation on Bootlegger Cay went from bad to worse. When Sara rushed over to Brightpath, Jeb Cady raised his weapon and took aim at the back of her head. He squeezed the trigger on the old western style revolver and the hammer eased back to the firing position. Fortunately for her, an ear-piercing bang filled the air and the pistol flew into the nearby vegetation. Jeb's hand split open like a watermelon hit with an ax, but that's the normal outcome when the bullet from a sniper rifle makes contact with human flesh. Major Sparks fired his second prefect shot, separating the pistol from Jeb's hand with marvelous proficiency.

"Shit…," Jeb hollered. "You blew off two of my fingers."

Major Sparks kept his rifle on the ready and walked toward the clearing with his head and shoulders showing above the brush. "Shut up and sit down, redneck," he shouted. "If you try to run, I'll kill you."

Sara was on her knees leaned over Brightpath crying her eyes out. When Major Sparks stepped into the clearing, she jumped to her feet and charged in his direction. She threw a punch with all her strength, but Sparks grabbed her fist with one hand and spun her around. He wrapped an arm around her neck from behind while securing his rifle in the other hand.

Jeb saw the physical altercation and thought it would be a good time to make a run for the jungle. Major Sparks aimed the rifle and fired a bullet into the fleshy part of his right butt cheek. The shot didn't hit bone, but Jeb dropped like a wet sandbag.

"Calm down, Missy," Sparks told Sara. "I didn't shoot him."

Still holding her around the neck, Major Sparks

pointed the rifle at a palm leaf hanging directly over Brightpath. "See that bullet hole up there, that's what I shot. I had to dial in my scope. Thank goodness I got it right, if I didn't you would be dead right now."

Sara took a deep breath and exhaled slowly. Major Sparks felt her body relax. He loosened the hold around her neck. "It's okay, ma'am, just calm down. Get back over there and see how he's doing." Sparks let her go and she rushed back to be Brightpath.

Jeb yelled at Major Sparks. "You shot me in the ass, ya peckerwood."

Sparks ripped open a Velcro sealed pocket on the front of his camo vest and took out two small rolls of medical gauze. "You're lucky I didn't blow your head off." He tossed the gauze to Jeb. "Wrap one of these around your hand and stick the other one in your new asshole."

Brightpath was still unconscious when Sara got back to him. His heart beat rapidly, his breathing was shallow, and it was obvious that he'd gone into shock. The Major pressed the transmit button on his walkie-talkie and called for help. Agent Higgins heard the radio come to life back at the com-center. He dashed back to the console from the hangar doors. Captain Hawks listened to the conversation in the helicopter and interrupted when he heard that Brightpath had been hurt. "I'm on the way, Major. I'll be there in two mikes. If you're inland, you'll have to guide me to your location."

Sara looked up at Major Sparks. "Do something, please," she cried. "He's dying."

The Major pulled a smoke grenade from his utility belt and handed it to Sara. "I'll take care of him. You take this to the other side of the clearing. When you hear the chopper, pull the pin and toss it to the ground."

Sara hurried to the opposite side of the clearing. The Major started working on his injured friend. Brightpath told him about the spirit bag years before, so Sparks jerked the Kevlar vest open to look for the bag. "Christ, it's not here," he shouted.

Major Sparks removed the shoulder strap from his rifle and wrapped it tightly around Brightpath's upper leg to slow the blooding. He applied direct pressure to the wound with his bare hands and looked at Sara. She was looking up through the trees at the time, but felt the anxious glare and looked his way. Sparks had a look of concern on his face; he slowly shook his head no.

Sara's eyes filled with tears and she prayed like never before. As soon as she said the word Amen, she suddenly remembered that Brightpath left the spirit bag with her before he left the hotel room. It was hanging around her neck. "Thank you, Lord." She opened the top button of her blouse and grabbed the bag, then jerked the string to break it loose. She rushed over to Major Sparks. "Here it is," Sara said, handing him the brown leather pouch.

Sparks stared at the bag for a second and then looked up at Sara. "He told me about this thing, but I don't know what to do with it."

"Open the top and dip your finger inside," Sara told him. "Use the powder to mark a cross on his chest and then pour the rest of it on the wound."

Major Sparks untied the leather string at the top of the pouch. "I hope I'm doing this right, brother. You're the closest thing I have left to family."

The sound of helicopter blades overhead filled the air. Sara pulled the pin on the grenade and red smoke spewed from the pressurized canister. Captain Hawks spotted it rising against the backdrop of a cloudless sky. As he maneuvered the chopper into position over the trees, Commander Moore reminded him of what happened the last time they tried to drop down through the canopy. Hawks looked down at the enormous hole blown in the branches during their previous trip. He keyed the microphone on his radio. "Sparks, come in."

"I read you, go ahead."

"We tried this before and explosives went off in the trees. Are you sure it's safe?"

Major Sparks looked at Jeb and told Sara to come hold the pressure on the wound. The Major rose to his feet and walked across the clearing. He eased a pistol from the holster on his hip and pointed it at Jeb. "Are there anymore explosives in these trees?"

Jeb spit on the Major's boot and turned away without saying a word.

"Really," Sparks responded. He poked the side of Jeb's head with the pistol barrel. "Turn back around here and look at me."

Jeb stared up at the Major standing over him.

"Do you see these scares on my face," Major Sparks asked. "That ain't age, boy, that's battle scares. And it won't bother me one bit to make a forty-five caliber tunnel through your head."

Jeb looked up at the Major and his face displayed every battle the man ever fought. He could see that Weldon Sparks wasn't the kind of man to be trifled with. Jeb pointed to a tree near the edge of the clearing. "There's one more mine in the top of that tree."

Sparks cocked the hammer back on the pistol. "Well, you put it up there, so get your bleeding ass up that tree and get it down."

The Major warned Jeb that he had two minutes to disarm the explosive or he was going to shoot both of his knee caps off. Then he notified Captain Hawks of the danger and put the chopper on standby.

Jeb limped over to the tree and shinnied up the trunk like a hungry monkey going for a banana. He unhooked the trip wire attached to the mine and looked back down at Major Sparks. Jeb turned the front of the device toward the ground and started to pull the pin to set off the explosive, but a red dot suddenly appeared on his chest and he froze like a statue.

Sonny Blake targeted Jeb from the chopper. Sparks saw the laser and laughed. "Now loosen your belt and put the bomb in the front of your pants. And make damned sure that the explosive charge is turned toward your stomach."

Like Jeb, Major Sparks knew that the landmine had a shaped charge designed to explode in a specified direction. If Jeb tried anything funny, Blake would shoot the mine and the explosion would cut him in half at the waist.

Sara tended to Brightpath while all of that was going on. Her nerves were on edge the entire time, but the crying had stopped and her survival instincts kicked in. It wasn't her life that Sara worried about, it was the life of her love that weighed so heavy on her mind.

Major Sparks took possession of the landmine when Jeb returned to earth, so Sara focused her full attention back to Brightpath. His bleeding stopped, but she didn't know if that was a result of his blood volume running low, or a sign that the Native American remedy was starting to do its magic.

Commander Moore and Agent Blake dropped repel lines down from the helicopter and descended through the tree canopy. When they reached the ground, Major Sparks helped then prepare Brightpath to be hoisted up to the chopper. A team member in the helicopter activated the winch that slowly raised Brightpath up to the aircraft. As Sara watched him ascend into the trees, she spotted a white osprey sitting among the limbs. A cold chill ran down her spine. Sara wasn't sure why, but her instincts told her there was something special about the bird.

Once Brightpath was safely onboard the helicopter, Captain Hawks told Commander Moore that a couple of guys would have to stay behind due to aircraft weight restrictions. Moore decided that he and Blake would stay, but Major Sparks wouldn't hear of such a thing. Sparks suggested that he and Jeb stay behind while the others returned safely.

Jeb crawled to Commander Moore on his stomach and tugged his pants leg in desperation. "You can't leave me here with this guy," he begged. "He's already shot me twice."

Moore asked Hawks to verify his calculations. Hawks ran through the numbers a second time and confirmed that at least one person would have to stay behind. There was no way he could justify exceeding the weight restriction with the aircraft now being used as a medevac unit. Commander Moore considered his options and decided that he would stay behind. Sparks would return with the rest of the team and Jeb would be flown to the hospital along with Billy Brightpath.

"No way, that happens, sir," Major Sparks told the Commander. "The chopper might not get back until morning. You go with your men. I'll just relax here and wait on my ride to return."

Commander Moore shook his hand and thanked Sparks for the help, then he secured himself to the line hanging down from the chopper. Moore gave the line two hard yanks and he began to slowly ascend into the trees.

Sparks snapped off a quick salute. "Take care of my brother."

• • • • •

Agent Reichmann came into the airport lounge and found Abby sipping a glass of ice tea at one of the table. She was impatiently awaiting word from Captain Hawks about what happened on Bootlegger Cay. When Reichmann approached the table, Abby could see that something was wrong. "How bad is it?"

Reichmann sat on the opposite side of the table and reached across to hold her hand. She hesitated for a moment, but finally delivered the bad news. "I'm not going to sugarcoat things, it looks pretty bad. Your cousin has been hurt and he's unconscious. They're flying him back now."

Abby started crying. "Was he shot?"

"No ma'am, he was attached by an alligator. It bit his leg. He lost a lot of blood. Mr. Brightpath wouldn't stop searching after the injury and he almost bled to death."

Abby wiped away tears with a napkin. "Billy told me about some of the things that he did in the service. After all of that, I can't believe an alligator got the best of him."

Reichmann stood up. "The helicopter is heading back now. It should be here in about five minutes. Captain Hawks is going to drop off the search team and then take Mr. Brightpath to the hospital in Naples. Agent Higgins said you can ride along if you'd like."

"Thank you," Abby said between sniffles. "I'll be there in a minute."

Agent Reichmann went back to the com-center and left Abby with her thoughts. Her natural easy-going free spirit was feeling grief like never before. She stood up and tossed a five dollar bill on the table to pay for the drink. Abby walked between two rows of small airplanes lined up between the lounge and the hanger and tried to beat back the torment in her heart. "Honey Do," she heard a voice call out. She stopped and stood quiet, Abby hadn't heard that name in many years. Only her grandfather called her by that name.

She started toward the hangar again and heard the name called out once more, "Honey Do."

"Okay, this shit ain't funny," she shouted, looking around. "Whoever you are, show yourself."

"Up here, my angel."

Abby looked up and saw a white osprey sitting on the wing of a Cessna. "I only had ice tea," she said aloud. "There's no way I'm drunk."

"No my child, you are not," the osprey replied.

"Okay bird, if you really are talking to me, then why is your beak not moving?"

"I am speaking to your heart."

Abby heard the helicopter approaching from the distance. "Wait a minute. I'm supposed to believe that a big bird is talking to me?"

"We do not have a minute, little one. The time for you to do what must be done is now."

Abby saw the chopper come into view over the water. She shook her head and started walking away. "I don't have time to deal with this right now."

White Feather flew to an aircraft ahead of her and explained his presences. How the Creator sent him to watch over Brightpath and served as his spirit guide.

"No way, I must be hallucinating," Abby mumbled.

"Do you remember when you were nine years old and cut your knee playing football?" the osprey asked. "You told me on that day that you wanted to be a cheerleader."

Abby froze in her tracks. She looked at the bird confused. Little tomboy Abby never told anyone but

145

her grandfather about wanting to be a cheerleader. "Oh my god, it really is you. The legends are true."

"Yes, they are. Now listen to me. We haven't much time."

The helicopter touched down in front of the hangar and the search team members jumped out of the cargo bay. Commander Moore stayed in the aircraft to guard Jeb, and Sara stayed to be with Brightpath. When Agent Blake opened the door from the co-pilot seat to get out, Abby hopped in to take his place. Agent Higgins closed the door and latched it from the outside. He banged the side of the helicopter twice with an open hand to let Captain Hawks know that it was safe to take off.

The aircraft lifted off and flew away in a northwesterly direction that carried it over the Gulf of Mexico. As soon as the chopper cleared the mainland and made it over the water, Abby snatched the pistol from the Captain Hawks gun belt. She pointed it at his head and shouted, "Turn to the east, or I'll kill you."

Hawks looked at her and Abby winked. The chopper banked hard to the right and Abby turned the gun toward Commander Moore in the cargo bay. "Throw your weapons out."

Moore eased his hands above his head. "You don't want to do this, lady. This man needs help," he said, pointing at Brightpath.

Abby cocked the hammer on the pistol. "I said, throw your weapons out, and I mean now."

Commander Moore slid open the portside hatch. He tossed out his rifle and sidearm, then sat down at the rear of the cargo bay with his back against the fuselage wall. "You're making a big mistake. If we don't get him some help, he won't make it another hour."

Sara couldn't believe what was happening. But she knew that Abby wouldn't endanger Brightpath, so she just sat quiet and watched.

For some strange reason, Jeb got the idea that Abby was helping him escape. "This is so cool. I don't know who put you up to it, but thanks babe. Maybe we can hook-up after we get out'a here."

"Shut up hick, or grow wings," she yelled. "One more word and you go out too."

Captain Hawks knew that the wink meant Abby wasn't actually going to hurt anyone, so he played along with her little plan. "Alright girl, you have control of the aircraft. Where are we going?"

Abby tried to keep a straight face when she looked at him, but she couldn't help herself and cracked a smile. "Go northwest until you see The Trail, then follow it to the east and I'll tell you when to change course."

Captain Hawks turned the helicopter as instructed and lowered it to five hundred feet. When the highway came into view he followed it until they spotted the Swamp Ape Research Center. Abby told him to fly north until she told him to land. She took her cellphone from her pocket and typed a text message, then pressed the send button. Abby looked at Captain Hawks with an expression of deep concern. "I hope we're not too late."

As the helicopter flew over the undeveloped areas of Florida, Captain Hawks looked down on the most beautiful terrain he'd ever seen. He marveled at the miles of flowing canals, shimmering lakes, and massive expanse of unspoiled greenery. "This is breathtaking," he commented, with awe.

"This is home," Abby told him.

Once the helicopter made it over Reservation land, the Big Cypress Gift Shop came into view dead ahead. James Osceola received Abby's text and he was standing in the middle of the field beside the store waving his arms. Abby saw him and pointed. "See that guy?" she asked the Captain. "That's where we need to land."

Captain Hawks lowered the helicopter and when it touched the ground Abby returned the pistol to its holster. "Thanks, Rick. We could have never gotten here without your help."

Commander Moore shouted from the cargo bay, "His help? He didn't help, you hijacked us. You're under arrest, lady."

Hawks looked back over his shoulder at the Commander. "What are you talking about? Coming here was my idea. Besides that, you can't arrest anyone on Native American land. You have no authority here."

Jeb picked up on that right away. "Then I can just walk away, huh?"

Commander Moore glared at him with an expression that showed he was in no mood to play. "I may not have the power to arrest you, or a gun to shoot you, but I can still choke you until your eyeballs pop out."

James ran to open the door. Abby hopped out of the helicopter and wrapped her arms around his neck. "He's in the back, James. Is everything ready?"

"I got the wheels turning, but it's going to take some time," James replied. "The elders have to prepare for something like this. It hasn't been tried it in a long time."

"Please, James, get them here and let's get started. Grandpa said that we have to have him in place before sundown."

James shot Abby an inquisitive glance when she referred to her grandfather in the present tense. He knew that White Feather died years ago. James went to the cargo bay and helped Commander Moore unload

Brightpath. The two of them laid him out on a red blanket that James spread on the ground in preparation for what was to come.

Captain Hawks got out of the helicopter and hurried to the other side. When he rounded the front of the chopper, Abby wrapped her arms around him and gave the Captain a kiss. She eased her lips close to his ear and whispered, "Rick, I'm not sure what this is I'm feeling. I've never felt this way about anyone before."

Hawks slowly backed out of her embrace and smiled. He thought to himself how Abby was the most exciting woman that he'd ever met. She's beautiful, has a great personality, spontaneous and fun; the perfect woman. "How about you let me come back and help you figure that out?" When the chopper took to the air again, Abby didn't know it yet, but she was waving good-bye to her first true love.

By the time the police arrived at the hospital to take custody of Jeb Cady, the sun had set and daylight was fading fast. The helicopter sped back to Bootlegger Cay and arrived at last light. When Commander Moore dropped down through the trees he was greeted by a big surprise. All of the missing cash was stacked in a nice, neat pile and the unexploded landmines were disarmed and readied for safe transport, but there was no sign of Weldon Sparks. His radio was sitting atop the money bags with a handwritten note tucked underneath;

Thanks for inviting me to the party boys, but I think its best that I go now. If the Sergeant Major wakes up, tell him that he owes me a dollar.

Viva Las Vegas

Rite of Passage

Agent Higgins shutdown the com-center and returned to the hotel after hearing about Weldon Sparks disappearing. All of the suspects were in custody with the exception of Cletus T. Walker, but Higgins was pretty sure that he wasn't much of a threat to anyone. The case would be handled from this point like many others in the past; the FBI would just wait for Cletus T. to surface somewhere and then move in quietly to make an arrest. Higgins ordered Commander Tom Moore and his team back to Atlanta and he relieved Captain Rick Hawks of his duties. The assignment was finished in Everglades City.

Higgins took clothes from the dresser drawers and tossed them into his suitcase on the bed. A knock on the door interrupted his work. He opened it to greet the visitor. "Good evening, Agent Reichmann."

"You packing?" Reichmann asked.

"Yep," Higgins replied. "I have to pack just a few more things. Please, come in."

Reichmann sat in his chair behind the desk and leaned back to get comfortable. "So, when are they coming to move all of this stuff out?" she asked.

"Monday, I assume."

Agent Reichmann fidgeted with the items on the desk, first the stapler, then the tape dispenser, and finally she made a chain with paperclips. Higgins watched through of the corner of his eye. He could tell that something was on her mind. "What's bothering you, Agent Reichmann?"

"It's Friday, so we really don't have to be back to Miami until Monday morning. And, I was thinking that you never made it over to the Oyster House."

Higgins continued packing. "Go on…"

"It would be a shame if you didn't get a chance to visit the best restaurant in town," Reichmann remarked. "Their seafood is tremendous, and the drink specials are awesome."

Agent Higgins stopped packing and looked at her. "Instead of beating around the bush, why don't you ask me to have dinner with you?"

Reichmann huffed, "Jezz, Elroy, why are men so damned naive about women? I'm not just asking you to have dinner, I'm asking you to stay here and spend the weekend with me."

Higgins stopped packing to consider the offer. He suddenly realized that the pain that kept him from seeking female companionship in the past was now gone. There was no more pining for Sara, no more aching in his soul, and no reason whatsoever to pass on such a delightful invitation. The brief encounters that they shared over the past few days made him feel good again, but Elroy Higgins had been out of the romantic loop for a long time. He picked up the receiver from the bedside telephone and pressed three buttons.

"Front desk, how my I help you?"

"This is Special Agent Elroy Higgins in room 102. I want you to close out the bill for the week. The Bureau will no longer need the use your facilities, but I'll be staying for the weekend, so let me give you a personal credit card number to cover the charges."

● ● ● ● ●

Scarlett pulled the purple VW into her driveway and eased the car around behind the house out of sight. When she opened the back door going into the kitchen, her black Labrador Retriever ran up and stuck his wet nose in Cletus T.s' crotch. Smokey was always a

151

friendly dog, but he ate some wild mushrooms back in the summer and hadn't been right ever since. After the poor animal ingested the biological hallucinogen, Scarlett had to stop watching one of her favorite television show, because the dog developed a tremendous fear of Oprah Winfrey. Every time Smokey saw Oprah on TV, he hunkered down right in front of the screen and took a big dump, then ran to the power outlet where the television was plugged in and barked until the show was over.

"Can you get your dog, please?" Cletus T. pleaded.

Scarlett grabbed Smokey's collar and pulled him away. "Sorry about that, but don't worry, he won't hurt you. Come in and make yourself at home."

Cletus T. took her invitation to heart. He went directly to the refrigerator and opened it to look inside. "Ya got any beer?"

"No, but I can go get some," Scarlett offered. "Why don't you jump in the shower and I'll run to the market?"

Cletus T. raised his right arm to sniff his pit. "Yeah, that sounds good. I am a little gamey, I reckon."

Scarlett left and Cletus T. took his first hot shower in over a week. He just stood there in the steamy water and thought to himself that it actually felt better than sex. Cletus T. closed his eyes and dreamed of how good that ice cold beer was going to taste when Scarlett got back, but he had no idea that she made a mistake that could very well cost him his freedom.

Scarlett called her Uncle Beavis during the drive and told him the story about Cletus T. using his name. When she mentioned the heist, that was all that Bevis needed to hear. Being a lowlife criminal that would sell out his own mother for the right price, the Daytona based fugitive promptly contacted the Volusia County

District Attorney to make a deal. He would lead authorities to the casino caper ringleader in exchange for dropping the pending larceny charge.

● ● ● ● ●

Residents of the reservation gathered in front of the general store and the folks inside had no idea why. When Brooke Clearwater saw all of the commotion outside, she went to the little office in the back of the store and interrupted her husband's meeting with Austin Decker. About fifty people gathered by the time Rance Clearwater came out of the store to see what was going on. A young boy emerged from the group and told him that Billy Brightpath was dying, and the tribal elders would be performing a ceremony to save his life.

Rance laughed and shook his head. "When are you people going to start living in the modern world?" Then he turned his back on them and went inside the store.

A pickup truck sped by the crowd. It pulled alongside the flagpole in the center of the Reservation business district and four men got out. They unloaded a large tree trunk from the bed, then rolled it into place directly below the American flag flying overhead. The people in front of the store made their way to the tree and those related to Brightpath stepped forward. All told, three men, two boys, and four women stepped out from the gathering. They sat on the log facing east, then stripped themselves of all clothing above the waist. The women untied their hair to let it hang loose over their breast. Each man made a shallow diagonal cut across his chest with a knife, and the boys mimicked the ritual with their fingertips. The reservation medicine man stepped from the crowd to bless them and sprinkle water on their heads. It was going to be a long night for members of the Brightpath family. Seminole tradition demands that they sit on the log and pray for the dying loved one until the sun rises the following morning.

Back at the Big Cypress gift shop, James Osceola situated Brightpath on the blanket as prescribed by Seminole tradition. He tied a red bandana around Brightpath's neck and put a piece of charred wood in his left hand. Lastly, James placed the bone handle hunting knife in Brightpath's right hand and wrapped the blanket securely around him. James fired a rifle over his head to arouse the gods. He began a native dance around his dying friend and called out a primitive chant to the sky. James then scattered bay leaves with one hand while waiving a torch over the blanket with the other, and thus began an almost forgotten Seminole rite of passage called the Ceremony of the Swamp.

Abby and Sara watched history come alive before her eyes. Abby never saw anyone perform the sacred dance and she had no idea that James Osceola was one of the tribal elders. She always loved James and considered him as one of her dearest friends, but Abby never thought of him as anything more than a crackpot who made a fortune off the visiting tourist. She couldn't imagine him being so spiritual. Abby saw the side of James that descended from the most revered warrior of their people. It was the part of him that never wavered from his heritage and ran rich through his blood.

The ritual went on for several minutes before Sara questioned the proceedings. Abby explained that the chant is a prayer and the dance a tribute to the gods, so they would help guide Brightpath on his journey.

"What journey?" Sara cried. "Is he dead? Are they sending him to heaven?"

Abby's eyes glazed over. "It's not that simple. Billy must be taken into the Everglades and left there for the earth to do with him as it wishes. If he dies, his soul will travel into the heavens, and the gods will determine if he can return to earth. If they feel that his work here is not done then Billy can return. The spiritual journey takes three days and he can only return if the swamp does not take his body."

Sara began to cry. "But what if he just lies out there and bleeds to death?"

"That's not for us to decide, Sara. According to tradition this must be done. If it is not his time to pass on to the next world, then the earth will strengthen his body while his spirit is on the journey. He will be made whole in our most sacred sanctuary, the Everglades."

The Seminoles spiritual connection with the Everglades evolved as the result of a vicious battle back in 1835. Just before Christmas that year, President Andrew Jackson decided that he'd had enough of the rogue savages that couldn't be rounded up and moved out of Florida during the government sanctioned displacement of Native Americans. He ordered a military offensive and U.S. troops were sent into the Everglades to kill every remaining Seminole. However, thing didn't turn out quite the way that Old Hickory intended. Of the five thousand soldiers sent in to annihilate the Seminole, only three survived, and to this very day the Seminole believe that God put them in the harsh environment to protect their people.

"We can't let this happen," Sara sobbed. "We have to stop this and take him to a hospital."

"You can't," Abby told her. "The ceremony has begun. If it stops now, he'll die for sure."

Abby hugged Sara to comfort her and explained the happenings. The bay leaves were spread to keep the bad spirits on earth away from Brightpath, and the torch was passed over him to scare away the evil spirits from the sky. The charred wood in his hand would protect him from the evil birds as his spirit ascended into the heavens, and the knife was for him to hunt food during the journey. The red bandana was a signal to the gods to let them know that Brightpath is a warrior and protector of his people.

Out of nowhere an unexpected participant swooped down from the sky and joined the conversation. White Feather settled atop the split-rail fence bordering the field and made himself known to Sara. "You are his love," the girls heard a voice call out.

Sara raised her head from Abby's shoulder and looked around. "Who said that?"

Abby knew who said it. It was the same voice that she heard at the airport. "It's okay. If you heard that, then you're going to be shocked by what you're about to discover. She then turned to the osprey. "Grandpa, please help Billy."

"I cannot," White Feather proclaimed. "It was my duty to leave young Brightpath at the mercy of the swamp during his passage into manhood, but I was too weak and failed him. My love for the boy would not let me endanger him, and now he must face those hazards as a weakened man. This is my fault."

Sara's mouth dropped open. "Is that bird talking?"

"Yes, it is," Abby replied. "I told you it was going to blow your mind."

Abby explained the Seminole spirit-guides and the bewildered white girl just stood there gawking at the bird. "Wait a minute," Sara said, "let me make sure that I have this right. You're telling me that this bird is your grandfather?"

"Well, kind'a, but not really," Abby replied. "Not in an earthly sense."

White Feather explained his presence. "The creator sent my spirit back to earth in this vessel to protect the one that must save our people. You are the one that broke his spirit, but carry that burden no more. What happened long ago was not of your choosing, nor that of your mother. It was his destiny to travel the road that made Brightpath who he is today."

Sara was confused when White Feather spoke about her mother making the two young lovers split. "How could you possibly know what my mother did?"

"I have been enlightened since my passing and now know all things that brought my grandson to this place in his life."

The tribal elders began showing up one at a time. First came Henry Yellow Jacket; the men of his family served as tribal elders since the first wave of Creek Indians migrated from Georgia back in the 1700's. Next came Clayton Wildcat, followed by Reservation Fire Chief Sam Bowlegs, and finally Edward Big Sky came up the drive in his pickup truck. This made the required number of five elders to complete the tasks necessary to perform the ceremony.

The chant that James started couldn't stop until Brightpath was ready to be moved to his prepared place in the Everglades, but it could be continued by another elder, so Yellow Jacket fell in step and began to recite the consecrated words. Wildcat stacked small piles of kindling near Brightpath's head and feet to ignite two fires, while James spoke to Big Sky and Bowlegs. After their brief discussion, the two men got into the truck and raced away.

Abby asked James what was going to happen next. She knew there was a certain protocol that had to be followed according to tribal beliefs, but Abby had never been trained in such matters. James told her that Big

Sky and Bowlegs were sent to prepare a place in the swamp, however there was still one critical task that had to be performed before the ritual could proceed; the Seminole Chief had to say a prayer over Brightpath before he could be moved.

Wildcat overheard the conversation. "Rance won't come. He knows what we're doing, but he still refused to help."

Abby pulled her knife and looked at James. "I'm taking your truck. I'll be back in a few minutes."

"No, Honey Do," White Feather called out. "There is no need for violence. We have the blood of our greatest leader among us."

Everyone looked at James. "No way, it has to be the Chief," he said. "That's how it's been done for hundreds of years and we can't deviate from that."

White Feather launched himself from the fence and flew directly at James. James threw up his forearm and the osprey landed on it. "You have no choice," White Feather told him. "The purest blood of our people flows through your veins. You can do this, my Chief."

Wildcat looked at James and nodded his head. "He's right, you can do it."

James looked at the girls and saw the pain on their faces. He knew that Rance gave up on the old ways long ago and he wouldn't take part in the ritual. James had no choice, he had to rely on his bloodline and perform the hallowed rites. He lowered his head and asked the Creator for guidance, then raised his hands and walked toward Brightpath. Yellow Jacket stopped his dance as James approached and began to recite the final prayer.

The fires at Brightpath's head and feet burned away just as the sun disappeared below the horizon. The pastel purple hue of night eased across the sky. James concluded the plea with a request of the one true God to heal his ill brother, or to guide him on his divine journey if it becomes necessary.

Big Sky and Bowlegs raced the truck back up the driveway and stopped near Brightpath. The location in the swamp was ready. It was time to move their colleague to what could very well be his final resting place. The elders carefully moved the blanket wrapped body onto a crudely made stretcher constructed of two tree limbs with rope woven between them. They gently lifted the stretcher and placed it in the bed of the truck. Big Sky got in to drive and the remaining elders joined their failed brother in the bed of the vehicle.

White Feather spread his wings to thrust himself into the sky. The osprey made a circle high overhead and shattered the uneasy silence with a booming voice, "Tonight the passage will be complete."

Sara looked at Abby with terror in her eyes. "Does that mean that Billy is going to die? I'm going with him. I have to," she said, then started walking away in the direction of the truck.

Abby grabbed her from behind. "Stop, Sara, listen to me. I love you and I don't want to hurt you, but I'll do whatever it takes to stop you. It's forbidden, you can't go."

● ● ● ● ●

Four torches burned bright lighting a small patch of moss covered ground on the edge of a stream deep in the heart of the Everglades. The moon hung low in the black sky and peeked through a stand of tall pine trees to illuminate the sacred place. Suddenly, the piercing screech of an osprey sounded from the darkness overhead and silenced the sounds of a million creatures below. The dense vegetation parted and James Osceola stepped through dressed in full ceremonial attire. He wore a headband made of leather straps adorned with alligator teeth and a long buckskin robe decorated with colored clam shells. His fellow elders followed close behind carrying Brightpath on the stretcher, they too were dressed in religious tribal apparel. The stretcher bearers stopped at the edge of the jungle and stood silent while James spread more bay leaves and prayed to bless the place where they would leave their friend to nature.

White Feather glowed like an angel in the moonlight. He dropped from the sky and perched on a tree limb overlooking the proceedings. "James has been taught well," he told himself. "But now he must do the hardest part and leave our most precious blood to the mercies of the wild."

The elders placed the stretcher on the ground with Brightpath's feet pointing east so his spirit would know the correct path to travel upon departure. They slightly elevated his head and backed away. Each elder placed one of Brightpath's personal belongings near the stretcher in an attempt to keep him on earth. It is Seminole tradition for burial party members to break the possessions of a departing soul and set them free of all belongings, but in this case, the elders did the opposite in an attempt to ensure that his spirit would not leave.

The final words were spoken and the elders departed, leaving Brightpath to the mercies of the Everglades. White Feather looked down at his legacy and wondered if the gods sent him to watch this because he failed Brightpath during his adolescent training. "Is this my penance?" he called out to the moon.

White Feather knew that he must now do what he should have many years before. He looked down at Brightpath for a final time and lifted himself into the nighttime sky. The tropical air was thick and the osprey struggled with each stroke of its wings. The strong bird not only carried the soul of a once great warrior in his own right, but now it was laden with the untold sorrow of a loving grandfather losing a grandson. The splendid bird circled the place of rest one last time and then pointed his beak at the moon shining through the tress. "This is my burden," he said with a heavy heart. "It should have happened long ago when he was strong."

White Feather soared away entrusting nature with the soul of his most beloved descendant, and just like tradition dictates, Billy Brightpath was left alone with the earth.

Stillness covered the land and even a nearby stream seemed to hush in homage of the occasion. The full moon broke free of the trees, casting a subtle glow on the sanctified piece of ground. As the earth absorbed the divinc light, animals bcgan to make their way to the edge of the clearing. Panthers, bears, deer, boar and countless other members of nature encompassed the area. The creatures quietly watched as Brightpath drew a deep breath and held it in his lungs. His massive chest expanded beneath the blanket, then slowly the air crept from his body, and the Everglades fully embraced the spirit of its last true son.

One Long Night

Sara sat in the passenger seat of James Osceola's truck crying her eyes out. Abby was a bundle of emotion too, but she wasn't going to show it. After the girls arrived back at the house, Sara paced the floors from room to room and wiped away tears. She stopped on one passes through the kitchen and looked at Abby. "I can't just stay here and not know what's happening."

"Do you want something to help you calm down?" Abby asked. "I have some great stuff in the medicine chest."

Sara looked at her through glazy eyes and sniffled. "How can you be so composed?"

Abby wrapped her arms around Sara. "I'm hurting just as much as you, but I have to believe whatever happens was meant to be.

"You just don't understand, Sara, you weren't brought up in our culture. Grandfather taught us long ago about the journey and passing on to the next world. Billy and I both believe in those ways, and I believe in Billy, so I have no choice but to pray for his return. If he doesn't survive, then I'll mourn according to our customs."

Sara continued to cry as she walked away. She went out of the kitchen and through the dining room, then upstairs to Brightpath's bedroom. When she opened the door from the hallway, a warm evening breeze came through an open bedroom window. The curtains parted and moonlight rushed in to fill the room. Sara closed the door and soaked in the surroundings of the man she loved. A glimmer caught her eye and she flipped the light switch near the door. When the overhead light came on the room filled her mind with memories.

The flicker that got her attention was the moonlight reflecting off a silver picture frame standing on the dresser. The photograph was of a young Billy sitting on the hood of his first car. His feet rested on the bumper and his legs were parted slightly, a beautiful young girl with long blond hair stood between his knees. Her back pressed against his chest as the two young lovers smiled for the camera. The lens caught a trace of the passion that lived in their hearts.

Sara looked around the room at the trappings of a down to earth man. A neatly made bed, a shelf filled with books, a small writing desk, and of course, the male required television sitting atop a small table near the closet door. She opened the closet and found few civilian garments. Most of his clothes were government issued. Other than two pairs of jeans there were three olive drab colored T-shirts, four black ones, a mix of desert and jungle fatigues and in the very back hung his dress uniform. Sara never saw Brightpath in uniform, but when she envisioned him wearing the sharp creased dark blue jacket and light blue pants her heart skipped a beat. The jacket was adorned with three golden chevrons on each sleeve setting atop three rocker stripes with a gold star in between. The left breast was covered with battle ribbons. Among those was the one that even generals have to salute; the Congressional Medal of Honor.

Sara left the closet and went to the bed to caress his pillow. Immediately, the first time there rushed back into her mind. She was only sixteen and had to sneak in through the second story window, but it turned out to be a night that she would never forget. At the time, Sara was much more a woman than Brightpath was a man, but his innocence made their first night together so special. He trusted her with all that he was and Sara

163

could feel that in the way he touched her. When their bodies came together, love filled their hearts and merged two souls forever.

While Sara mentally sorted through the souvenirs, Abby made her way to bed in a room just down the hall. She'd wept little and stayed strong all day, but the stillness of night brought her emotions to the surface. Abby cried herself to sleep and her dreams were filled with memories of Brightpath. They played like a movie on the back of her eyelids. She visually relived the good times and smiled in her slumber, but the remembrances were too much for her troubled mind to endure. Abby awoke weeping. She sat up in bed and buried her face in her hands, then prayed that the dream wasn't a sign of his eternal departure.

● ● ● ● ●

Back in Everglades City, Cletus T. slept peacefully on Scarlett's couch, until a vicious pounding at the door startled him. A loud voice called out and left no doubt who was knocking, "Cletus T. Walker, this here is the police," Officer Fife announced. The police car public address system woke up everyone in the neighborhood. "We know you're in there and we got the house surrounded. Come out with your hands in the air and surrender."

"Come on, Cletus," Office Rollo beseeched from outside the door. "Don't make me kick it down."

Cletus T. sat up and slipped on his cowboy boots. He looked toward the hallway. "Oh shit, I hope them morons didn't wake Scarlett." The words had no more than crossed his lips when a light came on at the far end of the hall. The silhouette of a large pissed off female appeared in the narrow passage. It grew to gargantuan proportions as she approached the living room.

Cletus T. was more afraid of Scarlett than the police. When her shouts filled the house, he made a dash for his life. Cletus ran through the dining room with the speed of a world class sprinter and headed for the back door in the kitchen. Due to the poor lighting conditions, he didn't see Smokey lying on the cool tile floor and he tripped over the slumbering pooch. The poor old dog slept right through the knock on the door and the amplified shouts from the street, but as soon as Cletus' foot impacted his ribcage, Smokey snapped at the darkness and latched onto a boot. Cletus T. went down hard.

Scarlett came into the kitchen and flipped on the light just as Cletus T. rolled over to look up in her direction. Smokey saw what was happening and lazily laid his head down on the floor to go back to sleep. "You stupid bastard," Scarlett shouted. "They said the place is surrounded. I have a child in this house and I ain't goin'a let you get him hurt. Now get your ass out that front door and give up."

Cletus T. wiped blood off his busted lip and rubbed the golf ball size knot that jumped up on his forehead when he impacted the floor. "Are you crazy, woman? Them boys want'a lock me up."

"I don't give a Tinker's damn," Scarlett declared. "If my baby gets hurt, you won't be going to jail, you'll be going to the hospital."

Cletus T. crawled across the floor on his hands and knees, then slithered up the inside of the door like a slow moving snake. He eased back the window curtains and peeked out. Seeing no one outside, Cletus decided to make a run for it. "Turn off the light."

"What the hell are you thinking?" Scarlett asked.

"There ain't nobody out there," Cletus told her.

"Fife was shittin' me."

Scarlett got scared. "But what if they're out there and you just can't see them?"

A rascally smile crept across his face as Cletus T. looked back at her. The two of them didn't see one another very often, but it seemed that each time they did, Scarlett always showed signs of caring for him. "Why do you care?" he asked. "You just threatened to put me in the hospital."

"Dammit, Cletus, you know that I don't want to see you get hurt."

"Just turn out the light, woman. I ain't goin'a get hurt."

Scarlett went to the refrigerator to open the door. She reached in and took out the remains of a Corona twelve pack. "If you're going to be on the run, you'll need some provisions," she said. "Here, take this."

The kitchen went dark and Cletus T. eased the door open. He stuck his head out and visually scanned the back yard in all directions, then bolted across the porch and vanished into the darkness.

Scarlett put her hands on her hips and shook her head with antipathy. "I wish that man would grow up."

● ● ● ● ●

Things were going much better on the south side of town. A scented candle burned in a dark room at the Everglades City Motel, and a mix of smooth jazz played softly from a pair of computer speakers sitting on the nightstand. Higgins and Reichmann were finally calling each other by their first names and the sheets at the little inn hadn't seen so much action since Gene Simmons past through town on his way to Key West thirty years earlier. Elroy tried to make up for all the years of abstinence, and Casey enjoyed every hour of it. No one had ever truly made love to her. The experience was more than she could have dreamed. A layer of perspiration covered their exhausted bodies and the candlelight glistened off her prefect breast. Higgins visually soaked in the vision of loveliness. He hadn't witnessed such a beautiful sight in many years, and she never felt such passion. Neither of them wanted to speak for fear of ruining the moment, but Reichmann subtly broke the silence. "What now?"

Higgins glared at the ceiling fan slowly rotating above the bed. "I'm not sure. I just know that I don't want this to be a onetime thing. You have no idea how much I've wanted to be alive in my heart again. You've made that happen."

Reichmann moved closer and softly kissed his bare chest. "And you don't know how many times I've looked at you and wanted to make this happen. I could tell that you were heartbroken, and I knew that you were too good to live that way."

"I was a fool," Higgins said. "I shut myself off from the world because I loved a woman that was in love with someone else."

"I know about your life with Sara," Reichmann told him. "She and I discussed it a couple of days ago. I can see how you could be in love with her. She's a good person."

Higgins wrapped his arms around Reichmann and snickered. "So, the girls have been talking, huh…? I hope I didn't disappoint, because you've awakened a hungry lion, baby, and he's ready to eat again."

The two lovers embraced. Their bodies tangled together like a can of Red Wiggler fishing worms on a hot summer day. Just as the passion kicked off another steamy session, the telephone started ringing and wouldn't stop; the romantic moment was shattered. Higgins answered the phone and the police dispatcher filled him in on Cletus T. Walker's second narrow escape. Higgins hung up the phone and looked at Reichmann. She was lying on her stomach on top of the sheets with her fabulous body on full display. The contrast between the rich dark suntan that covered most of her and the milky white mounds of her amazing bottom was indeed a sight to behold. "You don't know how bad it pains me to say this," Higgins told her, "but we have to go to work."

Reichmann jumped out of bed and teasingly ran into the bathroom. "Dibs on the shower."

Higgins smiled and put his one sixty four I.Q. to work. Cletus T. had already slipped away, so why be in a hurry. A little extra time getting ready to go wouldn't hurt a damned thing. He tapped on the bathroom door and announced, "Plumber, ma'am."

Some Things Never Change

The Brightpath house seemed empty and lifeless the next morning. As the girls slept inside, White Feather rested atop the red brick chimney standing high above the roof. Another cold front moved across Florida during the night and the temperature dropped into the forties. The cool morning air resting over the warm swamp formed a layer of dense fog that hugged the ground and made the Reservation look like an eerie scene from a low budget horror movie.

Abby was awakened from her restless sleep by the sound of roosters welcoming the new day. She sat on the side of the bed and hesitated before standing up, but eventually made it to her feet and slipped on a robe. Wandering down the long hallway toward the staircase, Abby saw light coming through the crack at the bottom of Brightpath's bedroom door. She heard rustling on the other side and wondered if Sara had slept at all. "Poor girl, I know this is ripping her apart."

The aroma of fresh brewed coffee brought Sara to the kitchen. "I didn't sleep two hours," she said. "Up and down, up and down, all night."

"Billy's bed is kind'a hard," Abby remarked.

A puzzled look crossed Sara's face. "I fell asleep on the couch."

"I thought you went up to Billy's room last night."

"I did," Sara replied, "but I came back downstairs after you went to bed."

Abby snatched open the pantry. She slid the can foods and cereal boxes aside then brought out a pistol. "Someone's upstairs," she said. "You stay here and I'll go check it out."

"No way," Sara replied. "I'm going with you."

Abby handed Sara the handgun. "Okay, come on." She hurried to the foyer and opened the closet near the front door. Abby grabbed the 12 gauge shotgun hidden behind the rain gear, then racked the slide to load a round into the firing chamber.

"Is there a room in this house where a gun isn't within reach?" Sara asked.

"Nope," Abby answered. "Stay behind me and make damned sure you don't point that thing at me."

Sara was frightened as they made their way up the stairs, but Abby was cool as a cucumber. She paused at the top of the staircase and looked back at Sara, her hands clutched around the pistol grip so tight that her knuckles were white. "Calm down, girl," Abby told her. "It's going to be okay.

"When we get to the door, you stand to the side and turn the doorknob, then push it open. I'll rush in ready to fire."

The girls tip-toed down the hallway. When they got to the bedroom door, Abby backed up to the wall on the opposite side of the hall. She raised the shotgun to hip level and readied herself. Sara turned the knob and pushed the door. Abby rushed in like a cop searching for a criminal.

"What in the world are you doing, Abby? I'm naked," Brightpath shouted. He covered his privates with his hands.

Abby dropped the shotgun and wrapped her arms around him. Sara saw him from the hallway and lost her breath. Brightpath hugged Abby with one arm and reached for Sara with the other. When she hugged him, he kissed her and held both women tight.

Abby backed away, but Sara wouldn't let go. "I thought that I'd lost you again," she said.

Brightpath replied with a hint of humor, "It'll take a lot more than an old gator to kill me."

"I thought you died."

"No," Brightpath replied, "I didn't take the journey, but I did become one with the Glades. Grandpa will be proud." He looked at Abby. "You know that I love you, but would you please leave. I'm nude, remember."

Abby giggled. "Damn, Billy, I've seen your naked ass more times than I can count."

Brightpath pulled the blanket off the bed to cover himself. "Yeah, when we were kids. Now, just go."

Sara flashed a sly smile. "Give us a few minutes, okay."

"Oh yeah, of course," Abby said, blushing. "I'll just go downstairs and make breakfast."

White Feather circled over the house with a joy filled soul. He flew high and fast and looked out over the fields covering the Reservation. "Rest my son and enjoy those you love, for the battle you were born to fight will soon be at hand."

Abby made sure to take her time making breakfast. She chopped potatoes for hash browns and mixed up the fixings to make homemade biscuits from scratch. That process alone took about an hour, but still there was no sign of Brightpath or Sara. Abby hummed and sang as she worked and occasionally looked out the kitchen window at another beautiful day. During one of those glances outside, two men standing at the edge of the property caught her eye. Abby focused her attentions on them long enough to recognize Rance Clearwater and Austin Decker. They were walking along the property line talking. The two men repeatedly vanished into the burned crop and then came back out in a different location about a minute later.

Abby couldn't tell what they were doing from that distance, but she had a feeling in the pit of her stomach that it wasn't something good. Just as her suspicions reached their peak, a helicopter dropped into view through the window and distracted her. It landed about fifty yards away from the house. Captain Hawks got out of the aircraft and it lifted off without him.

Rick Hawks paused to take in his surrounding, then removed his flight helmet and started walking toward the house. Abby ran out the back door. Her heart skipped a beat when the handsome flyer smiled at her. Captain Hawks saw the excitement on her face and decided right then and there that he was going to make it his mission to show Abby what true love is all about.

●　●　●　●　●

Agents Higgins and Reichmann spent their morning at the Everglades City Police Station. After the Chief of Police filled Higgins in on the information he received from the Volusia County District Attorney, Higgins couldn't believe that the local police tried to apprehend Cletus T. without notifying the FBI. Once the official briefing was over, the real shit hit the fan. Higgins threatened to have the town's police certification revoked and turn the local policing powers over to the county. When he finished with the Chief, Higgins demanded an audience with Officers Rollo and Fife. He chewed their asses until the fog lifted. Higgins was a master at making a man feel about as low as a toad's belly without using a single foul word. The poor small town cops never heard such fancy language in their lives. After the verbal onslaught, they didn't know if they had been fired or promoted.

The federal agents left the police station just before lunch hour. Agent Higgins was fed up with Everglades City, and Agent Reichmann could see the frustration in his face. She made a suggestion to ease the tension, "Why don't we go to the motel and relax for a while, then head back to Miami and have dinner tonight?"

Higgins grumbled, "I can't believe those two idiots tried to takedown a wanted felon alone."

"Let it go, Elroy. We'll catch up with him someday."

Higgins stared out the windshield at the roadway and contemplated her recommendation. "You're right. I was shutting down this operation anyway. A big platter of stone crab at Joe's would go down pretty good tonight."

Reichmann reached to put a hand on his leg. She quickly pulled it back and turned to look out the side window of the car. Higgins made the same play, but he didn't stop. "Nice restraint, Casey, but we're off duty."

Since they spent all of Friday night entertaining each other, neither of them had actually slept since Thursday. But that never crossed their minds once they got back to the motel. The passion fired up again and almost three hours passed before they actually fell asleep. Higgins and Reichmann started back to Miami a little after six o'clock that evening. As they traveled east on Highway 41, a man walking on the shoulder of the road caught her eye. The guy strolled along like he hadn't a care in the world, drinking a bottle of beer with one hand and carrying the remnants of a twelve pack in the other.

"Did you see that guy?" Agent Reichmann asked.

"Of course," Higgins replied, never slowing the car. "Why?"

Reichmann got Higgins' briefcase from the back seat and opened it. She got the Cletus T. Walker file and pulled out the mug shot taken during the drug arrested and held it up so Higgins could see it. "That's him."

Higgins looked in the rearview mirror and saw that Cletus T. never broke stride. He'd paid no attention to the car when it went by, but if Higgins stopped or did a U-turn in the middle of the road, it would surely raise his suspicions. "This road is straight as an arrow," Higgins remarked. "How can we get back to this guy without spooking him?"

Agent Reichmann quickly came up with a plan. "There's nothing between him and Ochopee. Since he's walking in that direction, he has to be going there. Why don't we just go to the post office and wait for him."

The Ochopee post office was only a half a mile ahead. There was nothing along the road but wilderness between Cletus T. and the tiny building. Agent Higgins looked at Reichmann and smiled. "This guy has already slipped away twice. It would only be fitting if he just walked right up to us in the middle of nowhere."

Reichmann stated the obvious, "But we'll be taking the chance that he gets away again."

Higgins pushed the accelerator to the floor and Cletus T. got smaller in the rearview mirror. "Let me tell you something that you'll soon discover about me, Casey. I sometimes like to play a little cat and mouse game with the people that we're looking for. It kind of makes me feel like Pat Garrett tracking Billy the Kid."

"I'm seeing a side of you that I never imagined," Reichmann replied. "I like it."

Cletus T. meandered along the roadside enjoying the wonders of nature and sipped on a warm bottle of his favorite beverage. He saw a nice couple sitting on a bench in front of the post office and approached them with a friendly smile. "Excuse me folks, you wouldn't happen to be goin' to Miami, would ya?"

Higgins stood up and answered cheerfully. "Yes sir, we sure are. Would you like a lift?"

"Boy, I sure would," Cletus T. replied. "I've been walking since late last night. My feet are killin' me. Beavis is the name, Beavis Wilkes."

"Nice to meet you, sir," Higgins responded. "This is Casey Reichmann, and my name is Elroy Higgins. We work for the FBI and you're under arrest, Mr. Walker."

Cletus T. knew that the gig was up. Reichmann had sneaked around behind him while he spoke to Higgins. She pressed her gun barrel against the base of his skull. Cletus T. dropped the beer and ended his weeklong plight with a single word that pretty much summed up the entire adventure, "Shit!"

● ● ● ● ●

The day was winding down in grand fashion; Agent Higgins got his man, and the Brightpath ranch was abuzz with good times. The spirit bag worked perfectly and Billy Brightpath was back to a hundred percent. He and Abby treated their guests to steak dinners, a few rounds of fire water, and lots of good music. The party moved out to the front porch after dinner and the gang watched the sunset. Brightpath and Sara enjoyed the porch swing, while Abby and Rick held hands and chatted in two rocking chairs.

As dusk covered the Reservation and the last traces of daylight faded away, a silver sedan turned off the State Route 88 and eased up the driveway toward the house. Brightpath saw the U.S. Government license plate as the car approached. "Rick, would you take the

175

ladies inside for a bit? I have some business to tend to."

The car stopped near the house and General Matthew Knowles got out of the passenger side door. A man dressed in a dark blue suit exited a rear door and the two of them walked to the base of the steps leading to the porch. They stopped on the walkway and looked up at Brightpath standing over them. From their vantage point he looked like a giant.

"Sergeant Major, may we have a word?" the General asked.

Brightpath looked at them and all of the emotion faded from his face. "I'm retired, General. I don't work for you anymore."

General Knowles always held a great respect for Brightpath, but even a man in his lofty position has to answer to others. "Please, hear me out Sergeant Major."

"You guys are like the IRS," Brightpath remarked. He pointed at the rocking chairs. "Once you get your hooks in somebody, you don't let go until there's nothing left to take."

The General and his guest sat in the chairs while Brightpath paced back and forth in front of them. General Knowles read from a top secret file and briefed him on a situation that occurred two weeks earlier. A terrorist organization based in Iran bombed the newly established American embassy in Fallujah, Iraq. They killed nine U.S. service members and eleven civilians in the attack. The same group recently acquired a nuclear weapon and they intend to use it on American soil. Military intelligence confirmed the location of the militant camp and its smack dab in the middle of an area that has only been successfully infiltrated one time in the past.

General Knowles closed the file and stood up to look at Brightpath face to face. "The training camp is on the palace grounds of Sheik Ali Achmed."

Brightpath looked away. "How did I know you were going to say that? Like I said before, my military days are over."

The man in the blue suit entered the conversation. "The U.S. government is asking for your help, Sergeant Major. I think you should listen."

Brightpath never looked at him. He looked back at General Knowles. "Who is that guy?"

"His name is Steven Menace. He's the new assistant director of the CIA."

"I'm here to ensure your assistance," Menace said.

Brightpath finally turned to him. "And just how do you intend to do that?"

"If you don't help, you'll be locked up for the Glades Corp bombing."

"Agent Higgins took care of that in exchange for me helping with the casino robbers."

Menace copped an attitude. "Agent Higgins has no authority to bargain for the Attorney General, but I do. Tell me that you'll assist with this mission, and I'll make a call that will make the charges go away forever."

Brightpath stood quiet for a few seconds, but finally answered. "I know you have other people that can do this job. All I want is to be with my family and live out my days in peace."

Menace replied with his elitist tone. "Speaking of family, if you don't help, Abby Brightpath will be arrested for hijacking a military aircraft. I think you may know her."

Sara, Abby, and Captain Hawks all listened from inside the door. Sara rushed to get her cellphone and call Higgins. He told her that someone in Washington, D.C. lowballed him on the Brightpath deal and the federal district attorney refused to drop the charges. He did everything in his power to help, but for the first time in his career, Higgins got no assistance from the federal prosecutor.

The egotistical bureaucrat made a major mistake when he threatened to arrest Abby. Brightpath grabbed his throat and lifted him off the floor with one hand. Sara came out with her cellphone in hand. "Billy," she shouted, "Elroy is on the phone. He wants to speak with you."

Brightpath took a deep breath to compose himself and then let go of the CIA man. Menace dropped to the ground like a rucksack full of dirty laundry. Brightpath took the phone from Sara, and Higgins explained what had happened. He apologized for not being able to keep his word, but for now the federal charges were valid. Brightpath handed the phone back to Sara and peered down at Mr. Menace. "I don't ever want to see you again, mister. If I do, you're going to know what a cat feels like when it gets caught in a fan belt."

He looked at General Knowles. "Let's go inside, Knowles, and talk compensation."

"That's General Knowles to you, Sergeant Major."

"Wrong, I'm not a soldier anymore, I'm a private contractor. From now on, you call me by the name that my honored grandfather gave our family, Brightpath.

Epilogue

The Sons of the New Confederacy received an array of sentences for their crimes.

Little Moe Gibbs and Boo Hawkins had their federal charges dropped after cooperating with Agent Reichmann. However, they did have to face state charges for burglarizing the pharmacy on the night of their capture. Both were ordered to spend eighteen month behind bars for that offense, but the actual jail time was reduced to time served. The presiding judge just happened to be Boo's uncle on his mother's side of the family.

Bubba Wilkes and Junior Selby each received a two year sentence in a federal penitentiary for conspiracy to commit piracy. Bubba was sent to the minimum security facility in McRae, Georgia, where he works at the prison golf course and is currently learning to construct custom golf clubs as a trade.

Junior Selby is doing his time in Beaumont, Texas. His rehabilitation program consists of working as a ranch hand for the prison rodeo team. They're not very good, but the warden is a big fan of the sport. The team members get furloughs on weekends when there is no competition, and they receive special discounts at the nearby cathouse where the warden's sister serves as madam.

Jeb Cady got the hard time. He was convicted on federal piracy charges and ordered to serve ten years in prison, then turned over to state authorities and sentenced to twenty-five years for kidnapping and assault with a deadly weapon. Jeb is currently making license plates at the state penitentiary in Stark, Florida.

Cletus T. Walker was ordered to serve fifteen years for the crimes he committed. Arrangements were made for him to do time in the federal maximum security complex in Coleman, Florida. When he was being transported to the facility, the prison bus broke down in the middle of nowhere and Cletus T. was the closest thing to a mechanic they had available. The lead guard took off his handcuffs and ordered him to check the engine under the supervision of two guards.

Cletus T. dug around under the hood for over an hour and eventually one of the guards went back inside the bus to get a drink of water. When he returned to the front of the vehicle, his partner was on the ground knocked out cold, and Cletus T. Walker was nowhere in sight. The guards searched the desolate area for hours and found nothing. The only sign of human life was a lady that cruised by in a purple Volkswagen Beetle just before sundown.

● ● ● ● ●

Elroy Higgins and Casey Reichmann went on to have a wonderful relationship. The job created a few snags in the early going, but Casey knew exactly how to take care of that. She came to terms with her heritage and realized that the Reichmann family did a lot of good since the days of World War II, so Casey stopped trying to right the wrongs that she never committed and resigned her commission with the FBI. She opened a modeling studio in South Beach and a very successful line of high fashion clothing soon hit the stores with the "Casey" label.

Higgins made a fortune as an equal partner with Casey. She begged him to give up his law enforcement career, but Agent Elroy Higgins vowed to never leave his position with the Bureau as long as a hardboiled criminal like Cletus T. Walker was on the run.

● ● ● ● ●

Captain Rick Hawks finally found a woman that was good for him; Abby is strong enough to keep his wild nature in check. Rick know that she's the woman he always dreamed of, and Abby fills his soul with the love that he'd longed for ever since being jilted. When Abby smiles, it lights up his world. She feels the same way about Rick; he is exactly what she always wanted in a man. Someone strong, straight forward, honest, handsome, and she can feel his love deep in her heart. Plus, Rick is the only man that could ever keep up with her in bed.

● ● ● ● ●

Brightpath saw an incredible opportunity during the General's visit. He knew that the feds paid private contractors very well to do a job like this one, so he made the best of the situation and secured his future. Brightpath asked Abby how much she thought it would cost to build the barn and stable for the horse breeding business that he wanted to start. After she quoted an extremely exaggerated number, he then asked Rick Hawks about the possible startup cost for a helicopter charter business. When the General heard the final tally it almost floored him, but he agreed to the price and the two men shook hands to seal the deal.

Sara and Brightpath spent two weeks together before he left to start the mission. They treasured their time together and made the best of every minute. He re-established his humble roots and did a little work around the ranch. Brightpath started building the barn and stables for his future business venture, and he constructed a gazebo on the property where he would have a peaceful place to connect with nature.

Sara took a brief vacation and dedicated herself to mending their relationship. When the day came and Brightpath had to leave for the mission, he left a little piece of himself behind that no one knew about just yet. Sara returned to the newspaper after his departure and carried on her duties as a topnotch reporter. She knew that Brightpath was on a dangerous mission, but Sara had no idea just how much of an impact she would have on his assignment. And it would happen in a way that neither of them ever saw coming.

Rum Runner Recipe

1 oz. Pineapple Juice

1 oz. Orange Juice

1 oz. Light Rum

1 oz. Dark Rum

1 oz. Blackberry Liqueur

1 oz. Banana Liqueur

1 oz. Sour Mix

Splash of Grenadine

Fill a glass with ice and pour in the mixture.

Optional:
1 oz. of Bacardi 151 lightly on top for additional kick.

Frozen mix: Put ice into a blender and add mixture. Blend to desired consistency then pour into a hi-ball glass. Garnish with an orange slice and slowly pour the optional Bacardi 151 on top.

Caution: **Consumption in large quantities may result in embarrassing behavior.**

27425292R00117

Made in the USA
Columbia, SC
28 September 2018